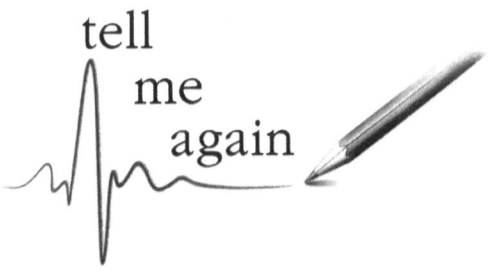

tell
me
again

Perspectives in Medical Humanities

Perspectives in Medical Humanities publishes scholarship produced or reviewed under the auspices of the University of California Medical Humanities Consortium, a multi-campus collaborative of faculty, students and trainees in the humanities, medicine, and health sciences. Our series invites scholars from the humanities and health care professions to share narratives and analysis on health, healing, and the contexts of our beliefs and practices that impact biomedical inquiry.

General Editor

Brian Dolan, PhD, Professor of Social Medicine and Medical Humanities, University of California, San Francisco (UCSF)

Recent Titles

Clowns and Jokers Can Heal Us: Comedy and Medicine
By Albert Howard Carter III (Fall 2011)

The Remarkables: Endocrine Abnormalities in Art
By Carol Clark and Orlo Clark (Winter 2011)

Health Citizenship: Essays in Social Medicine and Biomedical Politics
By Dorothy Porter (Winter 2011)

What to Read on Love, not Sex: Freud, Fiction, and the Articulation
of Truth in Modern Psychological Science
By Edison Miyawaki, MD; Foreword by Harold Bloom (Fall 2012)

Patient Poets: Illness from Inside Out
By Marilyn Chandler McEntyre (Spring 2013)

www.UCMedicalHumanitiesPress.com

brian.dolan@ucsf.edu

This series is made possible by the generous support of the Dean of the School of Medicine at UCSF, the Center for Humanities and Health Sciences at UCSF, and a Multi-Campus Research Program Grant from the University of California Office of the President.

tell me again

Poetry and Prose from
The Healing Art of Writing, 2012

EDITED BY
Joan Baranow, PhD
David Watts, MD

First published in 2014
University of California Medical Humanities Press in partnership with
California Digital Library
San Francisco - Berkeley

© 2014
University of California
Medical Humanities Consortium
3333 California Street, Suite 485
San Francisco, CA 94143-0850

Designed by Lesley Benedict

Library of Congress Control Number: 2013957683

ISBN 978-0-9889865-3-4

Printed in USA

Table *of* Contents

TERRI MASON

Kindly remove your shoes

Kindly remove your shoes as you enter the forest.
Everyone here knows your name.
It's not formal, just necessary.
Make yourself at home among the roots.
We've been waiting for you.

You were homeless in your parents' house,
Jobless at work. What do you have to lose
besides everything you have known?
No questions of like or dislike here,
only deep engines without machines.

Come join us, we provide shelter
between rocks and hard places.
Here leaves lie down, become soil.
Leave your worries on the doorstep
and dream a blue dream for time being.

Strong Medicine

When they tell me to do my laundry separately,
because chemicals will leak out in my clothes,
I know I am taking strong medicine.

I think of my copal wood snake with the lump
in her middle. She reminds me that anything can
be swallowed and transformed.

Normal shifts along a spectrum of extremes. An IV
pole has become my companion, portable asp
tethered to my breast by two needle fangs.

One drug rubies, toxic to the heart.
The other, clear silent, discovered at war
kills tumors along with soldiers.

Both seep into my blood as I watch TV,
eat dinner, walk through the halls.
Yet all feels safe, familiar.

This journey I'm taking that will not repeat.

Themes

scar

A dry riverbed
traces the ancient channel
pink cliffs rise from the gorge

chemo

Great dieoffs and rebirths
herds of cells flee
lava from the volcano

hospital

Beached on high white sheets
night long rustlings, air in line alarms
snores of my roommate

memorial

Wish I could turn
to Ann and ask what
she thinks of the speeches

dream

When the wildebeest lunges
I struggle between the impulse
to run or to engage

home

My hair is growing back
the pink naked ladies
bloom in late summer

DAVID SCRONCE

My Eden

I give you this spider's web
Glinting from a tree.
I give your neck a rub,
I cover your back with lotion,
I lay you in the sun. A little heat.
I give you a glass of water, a quiet walk,
A dog, or a cat, take your pick.
If you prefer, a svelte giraffe.
I give you mountains, marshes, wading birds,
The laughter of plumage you barely recognize.
I give you shantytowns of tin
With wild shebangs for drinking in.
I give you Ko Un, Gerald Stern,
Every book I love, every line I've learned.
I give you drapery, or none,
An empty room for dancing in.
I give you a drum, a violin,
A troupe of players wandering
Your narrow streets, serenading.
I give you rivers and shores, teeming avenues,
Walt Whitman. I never give you war.
I give you orchards, walled gardens,
Stone fruit in season, citrus after.
I give you bread and water.

In a New Place

However beautiful, you don't feel safe.
You marvel at the rhododendrons, the prostrate bamboo.
Still, a shyness comes over you,
Awkward when you greet an asking face.
You want to take a swim but first you drive
To buy a bigger bathing suit.
Would more coverage make you less conspicuous?
Lots of local families at the pool.
You swim your laps but don't relax.
Heading for the showers, some boys follow you
Followed by their father, who hustles them
"You can shower at home."
Dressed, you think you'll take a different route.
A neighbor's boxer blocks your path.
You're grateful for her grip upon the leash.
You find you've circled back,
A pre-scoped restroom, you know the tricky light
Switch. You're practically autochthonous.
Now to find a bench, a shady patch
From which to savor the afternoon.
You choose "Penny Jackson,
1938-2010,
Professor of English, Expander of Souls."
Perhaps the lettered dead can comfort you.
You press against the armrest
Until you feel your ribs are bruised.
Among the leaves beneath your seat
A glint, a coin, lightweight, stamped *China*.
Your luck may change. You pocket this.
It's getting hot. You move to deeper shade
And watch three silent deer mince past.
You lie down on your back.
Cloudless. Crepe Myrtle. Bees diving blooms.

I Walk Out to See if
I Recognize the Blue Flowers

As I round the boxwood hedge,
Of course, I think, they're poppies.
I know this is wrong but I can't find their name.
I stare into their open faces.
The closest I get is "Viola"
But that's the family.
My language faculty's deranged.
Three times in two days
Someone says "trauma" and I want to weep.
Whatever trauma there was,
If mine deserves the name,
Was long ago and chronic.
Some pinches, yes, some kicks and stabs,
What's now called corporal punishment.
I'd hide the scars beneath long sleeves.
When Mother was angry, I stayed calm.
School was some escape,
Until the boys grew vicious.
There's a blue poppy called Mykonos.
I want it for my garden
Along with these blue pansies.

JENNY QI

Letters to My Mother

For one hundred days after she died,
I wrote her a letter every day,
as I had once called her on the phone.
I burnt messages on colored paper
with glowing orange tips of incense,
rough to the touch like used sandpaper.
I blew sandalwood ashes to the wind
with choking, wet, ragged breaths,
gasping, as she had.

In my daily letters,
I told her about my two roommates,
awards I won at semester's end,
the book from my favorite professor.

I told her I would fold her cranes
from colored paper—a thousand,
as dictated by some foreign myth.
I told others I might string them up
and hang them as mobiles in my room.

I told her about the smoke alarm
I set off burning paper cranes
with sandalwood incense and candles.
I told others it was the oven
in which I'd forgotten my burnt toast.

I told her that the smoke smelled like her,
like fragrant soaps and musky carved fans
and creamy white gardenia blossoms.

I never believed in anything.
Now I believe in everything,
all the rituals of all the faiths,
and if I turn off the other lights
and stare hard enough at the soft glow
of incense until my vision blurs,
I can imagine myself borne back to her
in ashes of paper wings.

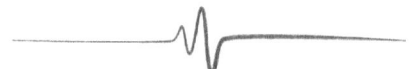

Playing Dead

for the poets I have loved

I lay my head beneath woodsy magnolia scent
and play at being dead,
let dirt collect around my elbows,
let ants crawl into my dress,
let my crimson scarf flare around me,
let leaves crinkle between my toes.

I think I would miss the sun's rough kisses,
grass prickling beneath my thighs,
and most of all your wild warm shadows
stealing into mine.

The Last Visitation

The first thing I asked the nurse on duty:
Can I see her chart and medical records? I'm her daughter.

Acute upper respiratory infection. Cardiac edema.
Multiple metastases. Pulmonary - 3cm. BM - 1cm. Glioma - 2.4cm.
The list went on.

I knew the answer before I asked,
What's her prognosis if she fights off the infection?

I stayed at her side while my father worked.
I read to her from books I'd bought too early for Mother's Day.
I sang her lullabies I barely remembered, arranged flowers
in front of her bed. I cut her turkey, fed her soup and soft bread.
I was never a better daughter.

My father, towards the end, insisted,
She want to live. She need get over infection. You ask the doctors
at the schools where you apply. Ask if can treat her.

The nurse asked, after I refused a priest,
Does she have a living will? We don't have one on file.

Sweetie, you'll need to fill out these forms.

Check yes or no. Blood diagnostics. No. Defibrillation. No.
My vision blurred over the words, over and over.

As he signed the forms, my father accused me of murder.
You give up? She want to live, and you don't let her.

Her eyes stayed open, unseeing, but her brows furrowed.
She thrashed weakly. I held her hand and hit the call button.
Mary? Is she in pain? What should I do? Morphine?
Morphine. I don't want her to be in pain.

My father's words, like a drumbeat.
She want to live, and you don't let her.
I laid my head on her chest until her gown was wet.

NORMA SMITH

House Calls

(fragments from the 1950s)

Jack Benny is on the radio. The hilarious laughter of the comedian's audience wraps my family in uncommon intimacy. We are parked in someone's dirt driveway off a remote country road. On Sunday afternoons all through my childhood we made house calls out to my father's patients—those who were too old, too sick, or without transportation to come into town.

Once on our way, out past city streets, my mother and father would sing to each other:

Put another nickel in,
In the nickelodeon
All I want is [de da, da]
And music, music, music

Or,

The prettiest girl
I ever saw
Was sippin' cider through a straw, ha ha

Or the song about the little boy who falls in love with a little girl and asks her for a kiss. Shocked at his forwardness, she snidely agrees to give him a kiss *"when the apples grow on a lilac tree."* The song goes on to paint a picture of the little boy waking up the next morning and looking out his window to see the remorseful little girl, *"tyyyying apples on a lilac tree."*

They were all love songs, and it was the only time I ever heard my father sing: there in the close space of the old Buick, with his young family around him.

They also sang slightly off-color songs that they had learned when they were stationed in Louisville and in some little town in Texas during the years he was training in the Army Air Force in 1942 and early '43. Something about a Sergeant Major making love to an Army nurse "around the corner, and under a tree." My mother was not worried, and she had nothing to worry about when my father went overseas. He wrote to her at least once every day, and she to him the same. I am now the archivist of his letters to her—she saved them all. Her letters to him are lost, somewhere in New Guinea, perhaps beneath the ruins of the field hospital where he and his company of nurses and doctors, clerks and engineers processed wounded soldiers from around the South Pacific.

Once my father returned home after the war, and with me added to the family, we moved from Detroit out to Central California. Like so many young couples in those years of expansive dreams, my parents were anxious to abandon the claustrophobe city, to leave behind what they experienced as the confines of extended families. My father responded to an advertisement of an elderly internist who was getting ready to retire from his general practice in Fresno. We were starting out new, with a life set up for us.

On those rides in the country, my father drove. My mother sat next to him in the front seat. My big brother—born ten days after our father left for the war—and I sat in the back seat, leaning forward. Our heavy automobile would lurch over trestles spanning irrigation ditches, past where the paved road ended, and pull up in front of a shabby frame house, the dirt flying up in a cloud, chickens scattering and squawking and dogs barking wildly at first but eventually moving stiff-legged toward the car, tails wagging tentatively. These homes, little more than cabins some of them, paint peeling off their walls, stood in bare patches among the fig orchards and cotton fields on either side of the country road. The dust that swirled around us on our way to a patient's house was the lightest layer of the valley's rich soil.

Once stopped, my father would get out of the car and walk around in back of it to open the trunk with the car keys. He'd pull out his great black bag—I was always surprised at its weight—and bring the key back to the steering shaft, and the three of us left in the car would settle in with Jack Benny.

My father would walk up the path toward the house, which looked as if it were growing out of the flattened dirt. The home was shaded by a few towering cottonwood trees in the midst of the field or orchard. He would knock on the front door or ring a doorbell if there was one, and shortly the screen door would squeal open and he would disappear into the interior, welcomed by his patient's husband, wife, mother, or grown daughter, or sometimes a small barefoot child.

By the time he got back to the car, 20, 30, or sometimes 40 minutes later, Jack Benny would be done, and it was time for the ball game. That radio roar of a constantly cheering crowd, punctuated by the crack of a wooden bat on a hardball and the announcer's voice, astonished and excited at every play, still soothes me. It is the sound for me of complete security in the heart of a family that was never so close as in the cozy nest of that Sunday Buick.

My Dad's car had a caduceus attached to its back license plate, to let the police know he was allowed to speed to the hospital in an emergency without being stopped. It also let thieves who were wise to the insignia know that there was a likelihood of a few vials of narcotics in that black bag. The Buick was broken into a few times; once, I remember, it meant that the patient he visited that Sunday was deprived of her weekly few hours of pain relief.

My father rarely spoke to us about his patients. I grew up during the 1950s, when fathers were not expected or required to talk to their children, or to show any of their feelings. We did understand that *this* silence was an ethical issue for him. Fresno was a small town in those days. But once in a while, when he got back into the car after a house call, he would forget to turn the dial to the game. The radio would go quiet, and so would we, taking a longer way home than usual. This told me something about my father and how he felt when his patients had fallen low.

MARISSA BOIS

Grandfather sits under Eucalyptus Tree

The tree sheds its bark in peels
without the hunger of disease
it grows. Stealing
light to feed its green
sucking soil to
quench its
roots.

At 85 he is a body folding
inward. Curling spine
gravity draws him
ever lower, back
to soil and
return to
seed.

I Press my finger to your Palm

I imagine
how your slender wrists
ribboned blue with veins
the milk of your belly skin
and the bones of you
82 years worn
will fit into
the black box we bury

If I held your ashes in my palm
how quick to scatter
grey dust then
then gone

Hush

He talks to her about
    their history of love
    and listens
    Sometimes the sharp knife
    of moonlight breaks open
    the dark

He reminds her
    of that one summer
    lusty in seventeen's sweet
    slumber and sitting in the canoe
    his paddles barely broke
    the water
    to hold their silence still

He tells her
    of this morning
    how in the yolk of dawn
    he chopped wood for their kitchen stove
    laid plastic over the marigolds to prevent
    their drown

He talks to her
    and listens
    to the empty space
    his voice leaves behind

NINA SCHUYLER

A Character's Desires

Desire.

It's a source of joy and also suffering. Aristotle went so far as to claim that a man is his desire.

Desire is also at the core of creating compelling fictional characters. But just one desire? Is that enough to drive a narrative? A narrative that is novel length?

"Give your character a desire." "Make her want something." "The stronger the desire, the stronger the impediments to realizing the desire, the stronger the story." "Drama equals desire plus danger." When I was earning my masters of fine arts degree in creative writing, I heard this and more from my professors and classmates.

While good advice, I've come to understand, it was only the beginning of understanding desire in fiction. To create a story full of meaning and subtext, a story in which the waters run deep, a character's desire must be fully dramatized on the page. What motives and wishes inform the desire? Is there a competing desire that knocks the character off course? Is there a motive that sometimes converges with the overarching desire, and sometimes diverges? As Kate Brady says in her excellent essay, "Captured in Motion: Dynamic Characterization," "Rather than reduce motive to a single explanation, the real problem you face is to compound motive rather than declare it."

In J. M. Coetzee's novel, *Slow Man*, Paul Rayment is riding his bike when he is hit by a car. He loses his leg, but refuses a prosthesis. When in the hospital, he is asked who will take care of him and that sets him yearning to have had a son. "His son, his imaginary but imaged son, would understand at once: pass on the burden, pass on the succession, call it a day. 'Mm,' his son would say, William or Robert or whatever, meaning, *Yes, I accept. You have done your duty, taken care of me, now it is my turn. I will take care of you.*"

By page 50, however, that desire has changed into an unreasonable passion for his nurse, Marijana Jokic. She looks after him in his apartment. She suits him, he approves. But she is married and has three children.

The desire for Marijana is a complex compound of unstable motives and wishes—to possess her to ease his loneliness, to satisfy his lust, to birth a child. His desire for her is stable only when it remains divorced and separated from reality. Which, of course, it can't. (Here come the obstacles.) Her family begins to intrude. She has a son, Drago, and he is a source of worry. He rides a motorcycle and she is concerned he will crash. Paul agrees to talk to him about the dangers and how it is to lose a leg. By page 72, his desire for Marijana has spilled over to her son. "But Drago, above all he wants to save. Between Drago and the lightning-bolt of the envious gods he is ready to interpose himself, bare his own breast. He is like a woman who, having never borne a child, having grown too old for it, now hungers suddenly and urgently for motherhood. Hungry enough to steal another's child: it is mad as that."

It's a short skip of four pages, and Paul's desire for his nurse has changed again into what he claims is love. "I love you. That is all. I love you and want to give you something. Let me." (He's offering to pay Drago's tuition for boarding school.)

A character's traits can help or hinder desire. Paul has lived alone for years. He's set in his ways and he has a fondness for what was once. He keeps a collection of old photographs, black and white, of the early mining camps of Victoria and New South Wales and some of the first settlers of Australia. He keeps the photos locked away in a cabinet. Paul's love of the old, his need for control, his stubbornness sometimes work for and sometimes work against his love for Marijana. She is from Croatia and wears a headscarf; she dusts his books, details that Paul likes. Yet, there are days she doesn't show up—family problems, family itself, which Paul conveniently and too easily dismisses: "As for the husband, he has not the slightest malign intent towards him, he will swear to that. He wishes the husband all happiness and good fortune. Nevertheless, he will give anything to be father to these excellent, beautiful children and husband to Marijana—co-father if need be, co-husband if need be, platonic if need be."

On page 80, Paul is visited by the writer, Elizabeth Costello, who shines a bright light on desire and its role in story, in life. "Do you seriously mean to seduce your employee into abandoning her family and coming to live with you? Do you think you will bring her happiness?" (She, too, will have her desire shaped and reshaped by conflicting motives and wishes.) Later, on page 153, she will ask, "Or perhaps your quest for love disguises a quest for something quite different. How much love does someone like you need, after all, Paul, objectively speaking? Or someone like me? None. None at all. We do not need love, old people like us. What we need is care: someone to hold our hand now and then when we get trembly, to make a cup of tea for us, help us down the stairs." And so enters the book, a new desire—the desire for care. Which hauls up the question, how is it different from love? Is it true that that's enough for an old person? Yes, Paul decides he wants to care, care for Marijana and her family and also to do good. "Before it is too late I would like to perform some act that will be—excuse the word—a blessing, however modest, on the lives of others."

"Your bleeding heart," she [Elizabeth] murmurs.

To create characters who engage and surprise, to create story that is layered, tension-filled, desire must be more than a single note, hit page after page. Desire must take on dimension, its wishes and motives teased out and dramatized. Desire must meet conflicting desire or be undermined by character traits and motives. Only then does fictional character and story begin to capture the complexities of human psychology, the mysteries and inherent tension of being human.

KAREN KENT

The Bowl

The therapist kneels at my feet
       gently and gingerly holding his metal bowl
       ready to give it sound with the wooden mallet.

"Close your eyes and listen to the sound
       as I lift this bowl in front of your body.
It gives me a reading of your body's energies."

I hear the high tones change as he raises the bowl
       sometimes fainter, then strong again
       to way above my head.

"What is this?" I wonder.

"The tone was a little softer around your knees. Let's try it again."

This time I close my eyes and scenes arrive in my mind's eye;
       a caravan traveling north through the Himalayas,
       costumed men and women of darker skin,
       strange smells—could that be yak butter?
       And sounds like I've never heard before.

The air is thinner here, to take a breath is work.
       Temples, healing lamas, paintings of demons and healers.

"Did you hear that?" I hear my therapist say.
"There was a second sound, like a soft Ohm.

Listen, I'll strike it again."

This time I hear the high sound and then,
the lower Ohm joins in softly.
Something in me settles, and surrenders to the unknown.

True North

You were my True North.
The sun, the moon and the stars,
the stuff of our universe,
guides for finding true north,
became the bright sun of
love and care we shared with the
steadiness of astronomical arrangements
of the moon and the stars.

We had a lifetime of 33 years together
when I oriented myself
to the love and care
we so freely gave one another.

In these recent years
my orientation became your needs,
the care I provided fired by the love in my heart
that grew over time.

At times I exhausted myself,
my energies clouded over.

Now you have left this earth.
My tears well up for the suffering
        you struggled to endure.
How hard it was to carry on in good humor.
I grieve that I could not help you more.

Now my struggle is to find
my true north without you here,
from this threshold where I am
no longer wife, partner, caregiver;
none of those.
There is an empty space
        in the center of my being
waiting to find its way.

DAWN GROSS

GI Bleeding

It was four months since my father's cancer had relapsed. Oral hormone therapy had failed to halt its progression. Bending to my mother's wishes, my father and his longtime oncologist had finally agreed to embark on a course of more aggressive treatment: intravenous chemotherapy. The day began with my mom, my dad, and me arriving early at the cancer center for blood work and a visit with the doctor, prior to my father's first-ever infusion. We were anticipating a long day ahead. We sorely underestimated.

Dr. Largesse was delayed, as usual, and his visit was notably brief. The fact that my father was in a wheelchair (not his usual mode of transportation) didn't seem to raise concern. The doctor's only question, "Ready to go?" was asked without waiting for a reply. "Any questions you have my nurse practitioner can answer. You'll do great." Patting my father on the back, he stood to leave the room, clearly not intending to perform an exam. "You'll feel better once the treatments start working," he said as he closed the door behind himself.

Before the nurse practitioner arrived I prodded my dad to articulate some of the worries he had raised with me days earlier. But it was my mother who spoke up. "How might we expect Roy to feel after today?" she asked, trying to anticipate the rest of her week and whether to take time off from work.

"Oh, he might be a bit tired," the nurse replied. "He'll only feel up to playing, say, nine holes of golf instead of eighteen." The smile on her face was genuine. My father hunkered down under the flimsy white hospital blankets.

"My husband doesn't even play golf!" was my mother's stunned reply.

"He's already so tired," I said, as calmly as I could. "He's so pale. He's been pale and tired and short of breath for days." I hesitated before saying what was really on my mind. "I think he needs some blood."

At this, the nurse simply said, "Being tired is not unusual. The chemo will have him feeling better soon." As she headed for the door she added, "They'll be expecting him in the infusion center at one p.m. Why don't you go and get some lunch beforehand?"

The three of us sat silently in the exam room, dazed. My father eventually chimed in and suggested we take the nurse's advice. "I'm not one to turn down the opportunity to eat," he said with a wink.

Making our way to the cafeteria, I told my mother I would stay during the treatment so she could go to work. "Don't worry, Mom, I'll keep a close eye on him," I said, distracted, nearly toppling a rack of clothes in the corridor as I pushed my father past the gift shop.

Mom, aggravated, took over the wheelchair as Dad laughed in delight. "Always shopping. We'll have plenty of time to come back after the chemo, Dawn."

My mother finally left us in the infusion-center waiting room, after coordinating how we would all reconvene: in which car, where, and at what time. My dad and I just nodded and said together, "Go!"—eager to be free of her tension and ready to hang out together, alone.

"Whew," he whistled once she finally departed. "She's a worrier, that one. She doesn't trust anyone but herself, with anything." He paused and looked at me. "I stand corrected." Clasping my fingers with his giant bear-paw-sized hand, he said, "She trusts *you.*" He smiled, and went back to his unconscious humming.

We were still waiting for his name to be called when he said in a mildly strained voice, "Maybe I should go use the bathroom before all this gets started."

"It's not a bad idea," I said, trying to stay reassuring. "And you're allowed to go during the treatment, too, if you need to." I wheeled him to the bathroom and asked if he needed any help. He graciously declined. I closed the door and waited outside.

Several minutes passed with no discernible bathroom sounds. I began to worry, and knocked gingerly on the door. "Dad, are you okay?"

A pause, followed by a tense, "I'll be right out." A few minutes later the familiar sounds of *flush*, running tap water, the cranking of a paper towel, then the *click* of an unlocking door. I opened it to see my father looking even more pale and worn, hunched over in the wheelchair.

I asked the perfunctory question again. "Dad, are you okay?"

"I think I'm bleeding."

Not the answer I was expecting.

"Huh? What do you mean?"

He shrugged, and I wheeled him back toward the waiting room, my heart racing like it had just leapt out of the gates at the Preakness. What should I do? This was my father. Who could I tell? No one wanted to hear the difficult daughter/doctor/ hematologist tell them their patient was bleeding! I'd already annoyed the staff at least once today.

I grabbed a nurse at the infusion workstation. "Did Dr. Largesse even look at his CBC from this morning?" I asked with the most restrained accusatory voice I could muster.

"I'm sure he must have."

I wasn't sure at all. Over the past several weeks, I'd made noises to my parents that I wasn't thrilled with their oncologist, but as my father had been a patient of Dr. Largesse for over a decade, they weren't inclined to change providers. I'd asked their permission to identify an alternate doctor: one whom I felt would be more attentive, who would advocate for my father and was closer to their home. They allowed me to schedule an introductory appointment, set for the day after this initial chemotherapy treatment. In the meantime, the infusion was due to begin at any moment.

"My father's pale as a sheet. Can you please tell me what his hemoglobin is?" I begged the nurse.

"Oh, let's see," she said, punching keys at the computer terminal. "Well. Oh my. That is rather low. It's 6.3."

I swallowed, holding back the scream of "He needs blood!" that wanted to erupt from my throat. Instead I said, "Can you please call his doctor?"

My mind was swimming as I returned to my father, trying my best not to show the worry on my face and fear in my heart. "Dad, what do you mean, you think you're bleeding?" I asked in a slow, carefree, sort of "just curious, no biggie" kinda way. My dad's answer was very matter-of-fact, articulate, and unnervingly calm. He explained exactly how things had gone and what he'd seen. It was as if he were reading a textbook on the signs and symptoms of a slow GI bleed. He finished and looked at me plaintively. "Do you think I can still get the chemo?"

I felt paralyzed, struggling to decide whether to tell anyone what my father had just told me. I suspected he might be anemic from a bleeding ulcer, not uncommon during the kind of treatment he'd received. If I was right, did that mean he shouldn't get the chemo? Insecure as a new physician, the thought of being wrong in front of my father's doctor—considered a world expert in our shared specialty—was very unappealing. More frightening was the thought of my mother's harsh admonishment: "How could you let him back out of this? I don't understand why nobody is fighting as hard as I am!" But it was the look in my father's eyes that kept me still. He had chosen deference to my mother's need to "do everything" over his own preference to let nature take its course. Knowing all the tears he'd shed in fear; wondering why no one ever asked him, "What do *you* want?"; remembering the endless tests and appointments he'd tolerated for the sake of my mother—no, the thought of halting everything, possibly for nothing, was intolerable. So I decided to keep silent.

The infusion was finally ready and my dad, though clearly worn, seemed relaxed as he moved from the wheelchair to a large recliner. I stayed by his side, trying to keep clear of the staff and to focus on opportune moments of comedic relief for both our sakes.

The treatment bag dangling above his head had slowly begun to trickle crystal drops of medicine down the long line of tubing when my dad quietly mentioned he was feeling some chest pressure and shortness of breath. "Like an elephant sitting on your chest?" I reflexively asked. He nodded. Oh God! Not this. I strained to keep focused—my head now spinning out of control. Casually frantic, I motioned to a nurse and told her of his symptoms. She flew into action, calling three other nurses to her aid in a synchronized ballet of medical activity.

One nurse immediately stopped the infusion. Another gently pushed steroids and antihistamines in my father's IV line, smiling and saying in soothing tones, "This might make you feel a little sleepy." Another softly touched my arm while passing my father a blanket. "How are *you* doin' darlin'?" *Me?* She's asking me how *I'm* doing? It took me several minutes to find an answer as I watched this flock of angels care for my father. Finally I tapped one on the shoulder as she fluttered by. "Thank you *all*. You are too beautiful and miraculous for words."

Hours later (or perhaps twenty minutes), Dr. Largesse made his appearance. Clearly unfazed, he explained that this was a typical reaction to the medicine and nothing to worry about. Unable to restrain my incredulity, I pointed out that the infusion had barely even traveled the length of the IV tubing. The doc paused for a second, then stated he would send my father home but wanted him to return in the morning for some follow-up lab work.

"He's bleeding!" I blurted out, feeling outraged and angry and desperately guilty for not speaking up sooner. "Have you even seen his labs from this morning?"

Silence. As he turned to the nearest nurse to ask for the labs, I whispered in my dad's ear, "I'm calling for help. I'll be just around the corner."

I slipped into the hallway, looking for a phone booth, praying for a large

"S" and red cape to suddenly adorn me. Thwarted, I used my cell phone to reach for the next best thing: my husband. Also a physician, but gifted with diplomacy and perspective, he quickly assessed the situation and talked me through our next steps. "Your dad has to go to the ER. Now. Get him in an ambulance and I'll meet you there." He spoke in the clear, steady voice I so painfully lacked and desperately needed to hear.

Twenty-four hours later—GI-bleed source identified as an ulcer, bleeding stopped, transfusions received, chest pressure confirmed as noncardiac stress, heroic cancer-treatment measures held at bay—my father was rosy cheeked and smiling. In the afternoon, when the oncology-clinic nurse called to see if he was still hospitalized and to coordinate his follow-up appointment, I shrilly replied, "He won't be coming back to the clinic."

Dr. Largesse never called to check on my father. Not once. As furious as I was, I wasn't surprised.

The excitement of the *chemo/GI bleed/are-you-having-a-heart-attack?* day clearly precluded the introduction to the new oncologist, so I called her clinic to reschedule, informing her staff that my father was currently in the hospital and couldn't make his appointment. Moments later, the phone in my father's hospital room rang.

I answered, my heart catching at the words from the other end of the line. "Hello, this is Dr. Venkateswara. I'm sorry to interrupt, but I'm calling to check and see how Mr. Howard is feeling. Is he available?"

"Yes ... yes he is," I said with a stutter of disbelief, as months of constrained guilt and fear melted into tears.

I handed my father the receiver, relief enveloping me. "Dad," I said, "we've just found your doctor."

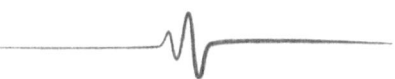

Violet

"Well, then why do you do it? Work so hard, work to exhaustion, if you don't have to?" An obvious question from a pre-teen daughter seeking quality time (okay, any time) with her mother.

"Because I love it. Because I get to do the things I like to do with patients in their homes, but to the *nth* degree." Isabell looks at me quizzically, and I forge on.

"Practicing medicine with the Palliative Care Service in the hospital, well, it's like home hospice on steroids."

"Why would you love *that?*"

"I get to teach eager and talented learners. *My* own learning curve is off the charts, and I'm asked to help some of the sickest and most desperate patients—all in the same instant." She has yet to yawn, look at the clock, or search the soccer field for any of her teammates, so I take a chance.

"Let me share with you one brief story that occurred a couple of weeks ago, over only thirty minutes' time. Maybe then you'll understand."

> *It was an otherwise typical morning visiting patients in the hospital—hearing about their nights, discussing any concerns, consulting with their nurses and coordinating with other doctors. At 10:50 a.m., I got a call from a frantic-sounding young doctor, an intern. "My patient, she's having a lot of trouble breathing. She's really struggling. I think ... I think she might be ... dying."*

Tapping into Isabell's medical knowledge, gleaned from watching multiple reruns of Emergency, I check in. "You know how there's a code team in the hospital for when a patient stops breathing or his or her heart stops beating? I'm on a crash team of sorts...we just crash differently." Her intense stare encourages me to continue.

> *Diverting straight down to the ICU, we found Violet, a seventy-something woman with white wavy hair lying in bed. I saw that*

her eyes were already glassy, a clear indication of a point of no return. She was gasping for air like a goldfish forgotten on a table next to its tank. Most striking about this scene wasn't the paleness of her skin or the ominous beeps emanating from her room. It was seeing her all alone. Other medical staff were standing outside the open sliding-glass doors. No one was inside. The intern, tucked outside one door, was clutching his phone, waiting for his supervising physician to pick up. The ICU nurses were hovering over the vital-sign chart in front of the other door. But where Violet lay, no one dared trespass —until we, the palliative-care team, charged in and fanned out instinctively, surrounding her bed. I went to her right side and placed one hand on her right arm and the other over her heart, saying, "You're not alone. We're going to make your breathing easier now." Without leaving her side, I turned to the one male doctor on our team—he was closest to completing his training, but farthest from the patient's bed and nearest a computer monitor—and called out, "We need whatever opioid is immediately available."

I open my eyes, as I've been reliving this moment, and refocus on Isabell. Her eyes are wide, unblinking. Her mouth agape. "What's opioid?"

"That's really strong medicine to help her feel comfortable." Amazed she's still listening, I continue.

We were six on the team—myself, our chaplain in training, two doctors in training, and two medical students. The young chaplain reflexively began to move away from Violet, anticipating a need for more medical personnel to enter into the space, but I reached out and grabbed her arm. "You I need right up here," I said, bringing her back up to the head of Violet's bed. "You're the most important person in the room for her."

Standing now opposite me, the chaplain held Violet's left hand and began speaking in soothing tones, like a mother to her child. "You are surrounded by love. You are surrounded by two—no, three mother forces."

Our youngest doctor-in-training—a mother of a five-year-old and an eight-month-old, the look of compassion intensified by the headscarf framing her face—occupied the space at the foot of the bed. I leaned into Violet's body, the back of my white coat's embroidered angel wings just barely visible. Our chaplain continued to stroke and soothe Violet's head and face with her touch and her words as we each hovered close and witnessed the grace in the moment.

Isabell waits intently, her eyes on mine.

"The whole time," I tell her, "the intern was glued to his phone outside the room. I met with him the next week, to learn what that moment was like for him. He told me he felt scared, isolated, and uncertain what to do."

My daughter, never having seen a doctor on *Emergency* not know exactly what to do, asks me to explain.

"Many doctors, new and experienced alike, feel this way when their patients are approaching death—including your father." She ponders this thought as I continue. "But this young intern, in the midst of his own self-doubt, in fact did know what to do."

"What?"

"He knew he could call for help. That's something I work very hard to reinforce."

Isabell nods in agreement. "What happened then?" she asks.

The nurses on the periphery seemed more comfortable. They began smiling and weaving in between us. They even thanked us for being here. Medication arrived, we stayed with her. Her breathing eased, we stayed with her. Her heart stopped, we stayed with her.

Isabell muffles a sniffle but doesn't say a word.

I asked the doctor still closest to the computer monitor to find family and call to let them know what had happened. He quickly searched the chart, tried making a call, then looked up at me. "No immediate family identified, only a friend not picking up the phone."

"Don't leave a message," I urged. "Just ask them to call the ICU as soon as possible."

"You never want to leave that kind of information on a phone message," I say to Isabell. "Imagine."

She shakes her head silently.

At 11:20, I left Violet's room to find one of our medical students fending off tears in the corridor. This was her first witnessed death. I placed my arm around her, trying to find something to say. This was important, a rite of passage, I knew too well. Remembering my first medical-school brush with death— being marched outside and told never to cry in front of my patients again—I took a different stance. "These tears are good," I whispered to her. "Never question that. This is sad, and you being sad, well, that means this matters to you. May it always matter."

The two doctors-in-training joined us. The young doctor with the headscarf was equally distressed, but angry. "I just can't get that picture out of my mind ... her all alone in that room. Everyone else standing outside ... but Violet, alone."

And then our male doctor bravely spoke up in this sea of emotion. "I would have done what they were doing. I would have gone to the computer, checked her medication list or talked with the other medical staff first. I wouldn't have gone to her bedside. It seems crazy, even embarrassingly obvious to admit, but it wouldn't have occurred to me until I saw it—that you can be with the patient and bark out orders to get what you need without leaving her side ..."

I look Isabell squarely in the eye. "Can you see how many people were affected, in those thirty minutes? Such a short time, and yet so much has happened." She nods but keeps her thoughts within, waiting for me to finish.

I take a measured breath and find myself wanting to cry as I share the final part of my story.

> *Violet's friend, I later learned, is part of an organization called No One Dies Alone. It's a group of volunteers who choose to sit with strangers, people without friends or family, when they die. This woman was so grateful to hear what we had done for Violet.*

"Violet died in our hands, far from alone," I tell Isabell, and as I finish that sentence I reflect on the possibility, with no family identified, that this might be the very last time Violet's name will ever be spoken, be heard.

"So, Isabell," I try to conclude, "this is why I do what I do."

She contemplates for a moment then replies, "I get it, Mom."

"What do you get?" I ask somewhat hesitantly of my literal daughter, who, when I said *"That's* what I want when I die" at the end of the movie *Big Fish*—meaning to be surrounded by friends and family telling stories—concluded that I wanted to be thrown in the river.

"*No, no*, Mom … Mom, really. I get it. From now on when I see you so exhausted from working at the hospital, I'll know you're okay."

"How?"

"Because I'll know you just got to be with Violet."

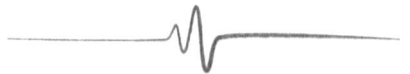

Mr. Rogers

I used to tell people my father *is* Mister Rogers—well, was. Not actually, but ... *really*.

His rituals of kindness and care echo through my own simple acts of everyday wonder—like taking off my shoes and putting on slippers each time I sit down to write, or changing from work clothes to cozy zip-up sweaters when I get ready to play with my children. I hear his voice, then see the world with curiosity anew—*"This is how you use a hammer,"* one of my father's great teachings when I was sixteen; his giggle of delight, observing spontaneous nail growth after eating a bowl of Jell-O; his constant, unconscious, beautiful humming, crescendoing when focused attention was required. Such joy in his presence—taking my hand in his, his fingers soft, round, thick as tree branches; wandering lazily in each others thoughts "eye" shopping, admiring antiques or art galleries, drooling over jewelry, and howling over tribal art, his awe of the colorful, magical desert animals leaving me believing I could dream wide awake.

Providing for his family brought him complete contentment and joy—his professional grace undeniable when I visited him at work, his soft, deep gray suit with soothing, silky tie; the mutual if slightly distant admiration he shared with the doctors, he with their papers and they with their patients; his office, no matter which Kaiser hospital, with its three constants: Jujubes under a myrtle-wood-capped bowl, a playful glossy-gray clay ram statue, and a green painting of a Trojan horse.

When he ran behind me on Hansom Drive, holding me steady as I learned to ride a bike, I could feel his grin following close. When, with elegant and breathtaking pride, he took my arm outside Touro synagogue on my wedding day, having earlier discussed my need for scuba-dive-proof mascara, he raised two fingers without a word—*Fight on!*—and in we strode, my father on one arm, my mother on the other, me feeling beautiful, proud, and utterly composed, my father, walking down the isle unpracticed, unrehearsed, gracefully traversing the central bimah steps without a break in stride.

His gentle wishes for simple pleasures inspire nostalgia—smelling jasmine on the wind; purring communion with the cats of our lives; asking, predictably, *"Would anyone care for some?"* when passing by a Dairy Queen, a frequent occurrence on family road trips, never stopping if no one answered, though he craved the simple treat of vanilla with marshmallow topping. His fascination with war shows and British humor filled nights with full-bellied laughter—sharing *M*A*S*H* and *Hogan's Heroes* with me as a child, "Hot Lips" Houlihan and Colonel Klink always sure to make him smile; snuggling in his velour recliner watching *The Benny Hill Show* or *Are You Being Served*: oh, how he loved the ever-changing color of Mrs. Slocombe's hair.

He would rise from the table whenever his wife approached, hold the door for all who passed, assist with the chair for any lady gracing the meal; he would bring elegance, beauty, magic, and joy wherever he would tread; he couldn't help but be himself, you see, like the startling beauty of the peacock—but my father, my father would never startle, and so, as I wrote in a poem for his memorial,

> *he became*
> *a hummingbird—equally as*
> *magnificent in its radiance, but*
> *so tiny and discreet—if you blink*
> *your eyes you may not*
> *believe what you saw—yet the*
> *radiance is undeniable and you*
> *know you have been in the presence*
> *of sublime grace.*

My family is convinced that my father has seized control of the air waves in the six years since he departed this world. Leaving a weeklong writing workshop, energized and overwhelmed—*too much to write*—I buckle into my car, tune on XM Broadway, and pray, "Dad, show me what you got."

"Be our Guest" rings out, nearing its end. I can't quite connect—am I Beauty or the Beast?—so I choose to hear it solely as invitation to keep listening as I slowly navigate the road away from Dominican. Five lovely gray-haired women, oblivious to my trajectory (not their fault; I am stealth in the silence of my new electric vehicle), exchange hugs with one another along with a bouquet of wild flowers. As the gray sea parts, a moment of static disrupts the connection, and I miss the introduction to the next program.

A tribute, I soon learn, to the life and work of Richard Kiley. I recognize him as the pilot in the movie version of Saint-Exupery's *The Little Prince*, my treatise on life—so I stay tuned. "I'm listening dad," I console myself ... I am listening.

A gay little love song I've never heard opens his voice to my ears, and Wham! I know this voice, this long-ago saint of the sands. I know him beyond that distant far-off land of plane wrecks and sheep and a heartbroken rose. I know him, I know ... but where?

I'm on a residential street now, distractedly close to the car in front of me, and then the "mad" knight enters, *The Ingenious Gentleman Don Quixote of La Mancha*. That's it! I pull over just before metal unintentionally meets metal. *Man of La Mancha* was the first musical my soul ever felt at the age of four. The lemon-yellow record sleeve featured brick-red letters and stark black caricatures—a fat man sitting atop a longing donkey; towering next to him, a steed with a long-faced knight on its back, lance in hand, plume curling from his helmet; and facing them, wine glass raised, a curvaceous, heated, raven-haired woman. *Who is that?* I was hooked before the first note left the vinyl. The story seeped into my marrow then stayed hidden until Mr. Kylie's resurrection today.

Listening to him breathe life into Cervantes, I feel my father's presence. *"I shall impersonate a man."* When Quixote begins singing to his love, a kitchen wench named Aldonza whom he reveres as his imagined lady-in-waiting—*"for whom great deeds are done, she that is called Dulcinea"*—my empathy for Aldonza surges like a tsunami of tears. *"I have dreamed thee too long, never seen thee or touched thee, but known thee with all of my heart"* ... my fingers ache in their search to touch you ... *"Half a prayer, half a song, thou has always been with me, though we have been always apart"* ... heaving sobs attempt but fail to obscure the serenade … *"I see heaven when I see thee"* … eyes swell shut … *"If I reach out to thee"* … hands tremble … *"Let my fingers but see thou art warm and alive, and no phantom to fade in the air…"* Imagining a cop pulling over to see if I'm all right, I try to compose myself, taking my curled knees off the steering wheel and removing my outstretched palms from the now fogged windows. The music pauses as the radio host reviews some historical curiosities and I regain my bearings. Ready to reengage my car in a forward direction, the ultimate soliloquy of the musical—the same, I realize, my brother read at my father's funeral—takes over the radio. At this rate, I won't get home till next Tuesday. I hunker down and wait for the storm to pass. And just when I think I can take no more—tissues, hankies, napkins, and sweatshirts soaked through, having now sobbed through "Impossible Dream"—the radio host moves on to *The Little Prince*. Make that next Friday.

Three minutes before the hour, soaked as if I just jumped into the Bay, I somehow manage to regain my composure enough to provide adequate oxygen to my brain and resume my drive home. I get on the freeway, approach the majestic Golden Gate, and marvel at the soaring towers piercing the endless billows of fog. Until, as if a foghorn penetrating the still of the night, "And now, before the hour is up, we will return to what was Mr. Kiley's favorite song of his career, the very end of *Man of La Mancha." What? We already finished that. We moved on! What do you mean?* At a loss for what this song could be, I brace myself and empirically pull onto the shoulder.

Aldonza, seeing Don Quixote on what will become his deathbed, implores him, *"Please! Try to remember!"* How could I forget this! Don Quixote stirs, *"Then perhaps it was not a dream"* … at my father's side four days before he died, *"I'm feeling stronger, maybe I should try chemo again"* … Aldonza replies, *"You spoke of a dream,"* and Don Quixote rallies, stands strong and begins to sing, before his final collapse … at this point I'm using notebook paper to soak up the tears. Listening to Aldonza transform into Dulcinea, I grasp why it must be *she*, the one who understands, the one who communicates wisdom, who sings the final lyrics of the knight, and in so doing, how the impossible dream, even in the face of death, becomes possible.

So, I stand corrected. My father, he is *like* Mister Rogers—well, was. But to learn who he is, *"Come, enter into my imagination, and see him ..."*

CATHARINE CLARK-SAYLES

Mercy
For Camille

The nurse had insisted
I must come, must "address a feeding tube"
And I thought of a conversation with a rubber hose,
"Monsieur, let me introduce you to Mrs. C,
she is one hundred and nine
and does not eat
in clear violation of Title 22."

To lose weight is a fineable offense,
easily prevented by a tube in the nose.
She had done nicely on brie
and baguettes—nourishment
for any Gaelic soul until one too many falls
brought her from her home
to the mercy of a proper dietician
and a healthy diet of bland, low-fat food.
Mrs.C ate little, then less. "So,"

I said, "We're worried." And she began:
The quality of mercy is not strain'd
it droppeth as the gentle rain from heaven
upon the place beneath, it is twice blest ...
quoting each line to the end ... *to mitigate*
the justice of your plea. She breathed.

The world needs more Portias,
are you going to be a Portia?

She got no tube.
She did not eat.
She died in a week:
her death, a gentle rain.

The Truth in the Room

Mercy hides in the hesitant pause
Stephen Levine

The truth in this room,
too cutting to bear; death
an abstraction, not likely soon,
for two of us, for one,
immediate and even life
nine decades long
will not satisfy
and I must guide decisions
away from what won't help,

hammer down the coffin lid,
but leave a little space
for a love of sixty years
and blessings: kids, grandkids,
important work and travel
to most of the places on your list.
The room is getting crowded
with all you have achieved,

but also we must welcome
your unloved child, your rage:
named after surgeons who could not
cut assuredly and medicines that failed.
Welcome her and gentle her
into dull regret but give her space to stand
with your list of disappointments.

Your oncologist says that chemo
is not working and you are sure
that hospitals with endless waits,
indignities and proddings from new interns
in their shiny earnestness
cannot be endured again.

I say "Hospice," watch your face
move into shock and quickly slip away
into talk of IV nutrition, Chinese herbs
and I say one brutal "No"
then wait again until the silence pains me.
I want to rush, to comfort you
with vagueness, promised time.

 As your wife pleads for something;
her eyes so shadowed this last year
but habit of sixty years
won't let her ask for help.
The clock ticks on while, outside,
my waiting room slowly fills
and together in silence, we wait.

Words Beyond Words

Words beyond words: your sudden wince of pain,
your indrawn breath, the tightening of your throat,
the way your shoulders rise, defensive with some strain.
You sit with tiny rockings of your body like a boat;

if you were I lion I would check your paw for a thorn.
If you were a horse I'd check your saddle for a burr.
You say nothing's wrong, you are just a little worn
from not sleeping lately and isn't there a pill to blur

the edges just a bit, something advertised on your TV?
An Rx jotted would be a quick fix: to sound out how deep
the unspoken river of your troubles might be
will make a slower passage as the minute hand creeps.

True healing comes from stories: the telling, the listen.
"Tell me," I say and watch your tears begin to glisten.

Burning

Lithium and strontium burn red
And calcium, though more the shade of brick

Phosphorous flashes pale green-blue
Zinc, the same color but a deeper hue

Selenium is azure, lead burns blue-white
Antimony glows celadon like a Song emperor's vase

Hearts, it is said, can burn for love
And faces flame a rosy shade with shame

Thallium, though deadly, gives light of pure deep green
Cesium is violet-blue; iron gives golden light

Magnesium flares a pure arctic white,
Actinic bright as it burns beneath the sea

I think that hate burns with a cold, no-color fire,
Darling, tell me the color of your flame

GINA CATENA

Aha!

"This is harder than my others!" Myesha protests, flopping long dark legs onto the bed. False lashes fan upon high cheekbones as Myesha's eyes rest between contractions. Medusa-like blond braids frame her face like sunbeams snaking across the starched white pillowcase.

"Kiss her between contractions to help." I encourage Frank, who stands motionless at her bedside. He smirks at my suggestion while transfixed to the televised basketball game overhead.

Myesha reflexively jerks up with another contraction. Glittering green fingernails yank her thighs yoga-like toward her shoulders as she curls forward to lean full force into the birth of her fourth child.

The galloping tap-tap-tap of her fetal heart monitor slows to a trot with each uterine compression, returning to its healthy gallop when Myesha flops back upon her mattress at contraction's end. The fetal heart rate slows from head compression during her strong pushes. As long as the unborn heart rate returns to his normal rate between contractions, we know the baby is OK.

As the Nurse-Midwife attending this birth, I encourage Myesha. "This baby faces forward making it harder to fit through," I explain from my perch between her open velvet legs.

With the next contraction, her labor nurse and I cheer, "You can do it! Great! Push like you're having the biggest poop of your life!"

Statuesque Frank continues to ignore Myesha's efforts. He absentmindedly supports Myesha's lower leg as instructed by the nurse while he follows a basketball game on the overhead television screen.

Frank's detached behavior makes me wonder about their relationship. While pregnant, Myesha refused to inform Frank about her gonorrhea infection even after she understood that the stubborn sexually transmitted bacteria could jeopardize her baby's eyesight if his eyes become infected during birth. Usually we treat both partners upon diagnosis, to prevent reinfection from a sexual relationship.

At the beginning of my 12-hour shift as the nurse-midwife responsible for Myesha's labor and birth, I had approached Myesha while she labored comfortably immobilized on her left side, nearly numb from the waist down with her desired epidural. Frank snored. His hoodie sweatshirt peeked above a white flannel blanket from a sofa across the dimly-lit labor room.

Bending to Myesha's ear, I awakened her by stroking her upper arm. Her eyes opened with a beaming pearly smile. After introducing myself, I whispered so Frank could not hear, "You requested confidentiality about your infection during pregnancy."

Myesha nodded, holding her blanket snuggly beneath her chin.

"We need to verify the infection is gone. That bacteria can blind a baby if picked up in birth."

Again, she nodded.

Still whispering, "I'll do a vaginal exam with a cotton swab to check for the bacteria. We'll block Frank's view so he doesn't know. We'll also draw another blood test for HIV. After birth we'll put a painless antibiotic ointment in the baby's eyes to protect him, just in case."

Years of practice taught me that low-income patients generally value direct blunt conversation about medical issues, even more than do my private practice patients.

"Thank you," Myesha whispered. Her full smile brightened the quiet hospital labor room.

As if casually watching an auto mechanic fix a car, Frank observed my exam with one eye peaking over his hoodie. That was a few hours ago.

Now Myesha pushes to propel this birth, but her baby does not descend. As the attending midwife, I would expect a fourth child to come quickly, especially with the strength of this healthy twenty-six-year-old woman.

Donda, the bedside nurse, monitors fetal heart rate dips which return to a fast gallop after each contraction. Precarious dips are typical for a healthy baby in a tight squeeze. The fetus can sustain bouts of oxygen deprivation for a short while. But if birth is delayed, the baby could be in trouble and Myesha would need a cesarean section. A healthy vaginal birth is preferable as long as the baby is doing well.

Weighing clinical options, I ask, "Myesha, would you like me to break the bag of water to help the baby down?"

"Oh, yeah!" she pleads.

"Your baby loses protection when I break the bag. In my opinion this is an appropriate risk now. I prefer to avoid a cesarean and help you have another vaginal birth if we can."

She nods assent, flashing her pearly teeth, "I don't want a cesarean."

"OK. We'll do everything I can." I nod. "You push with the next contraction, I'll pop the bag. It won't hurt."

Myesha again draws her thighs back, curling her chin and shoulders forward. My gloved fingers slide by her smoothly waxed groin, between labia through warm moist vaginal folds to the swelling balloon of amniotic fluid several inches into her vagina.

When I feel the fetal head press down into the balloon against my finger tips, I encourage, "Push harder. That's it. Straight into the pressure."

The fetal head fills Myesha's pelvis like a dam to prevent an amniotic tsunami from crushing the umbilical cord. Two fingers of my right hand press against the fetal skull behind the fluid-filled bag while my left hand steers a narrow sterile plastic hook up Myesha's vagina, pricking the tough balloon. Warmth gushes over my right hand, splashing over Myesha's buttock to saturate a white towel with blood-tinged fluid. The clean ocean-like scent is reassuring.

"I'm all wet!" Myesha laughs.

"The water's broken. And your baby has black hair—imagine that!" Still laughing Myesha asks, "You can see his hair?"

"Just a little. Shall I begin twisting his dreads?"

Myesha laughs again.

Frank glances disinterestedly around the room.

Myesha alternately bears down and rests while the fetal heart rate continues its roller coaster dips. Unfortunately, her baby does not budge over the next 30 minutes. My midwife options are diminishing.

"This one's never coming out!" She protests, shaking her head side to side.

"He's stuck because he faces forward. I can try to turn him. You'll feel a lot of pressure but it won't hurt through your epidural."

"Oh, please! Just git'im out!"

"OK, here goes. Are you ready?"

Once again sliding a gloved hand deep into Myesha's warm folds, my fingertips skim the fetus's scalp, measuring skull articulations. I flick a tiny earlobe confirming the baby's position pressed against her lower back.

"Breathe deep and exhale slowly. Pretend you're blowing out 100 candles," I direct Myesha as my fingers grasp the small head, like living tongs within her pelvis. The epidural relaxes her muscles enough to facilitate this otherwise painful maneuver.

My mid-forearm and elbow extend from Myesha's vagina like a third limb as I rotate the fetal head. Frank glances briefly then calmly studies a wall. Most men wince when observing this. Observing Frank's objectivity, I think to myself, *Aha! He's her pimp!* That would explain his vigilant presence mixed with aloofness. He stays close to be sure she does not turn him in. That would also explain why Myesha did tell him about her gonorrhea. Frank is her business manager, not her sexual partner. I wonder both what Frank has seen in his life and what brought Myesha to him. I make a mental note to order a postpartum visit with a social worker for her.

Early in my career a wise midwife once said, "It's not our job to fix their lives. It's only our job to get a healthy baby out." I sigh about human limitations.

Focused upon grasping this head inside Myesha's vagina, my aging back protests as my right hand stabilizes the fuzzy head and my left arm extends across Myesha's bulging abdomen. I simultaneously press firmly against the pregnant belly while internally rotating the fetal head. The unborn fetal head wiggles in protest of my grasp.

"Whoa!" Myesha exclaims, leaning back. "I never felt anything like *that*!"

"I'm sorry." I continue steady pressure as the baby rotates counterclockwise. "Thank heavens for your epidural. This is working."

Donda monitors the fetal heart rate drop to 60 beats per minute, less than half normal rate. My pulse increases in direct proportion to the dropping fetal heart rate. As we enter the fourth minute, I'm about to call for an emergency cesarean when I feel the baby lock into proper position, having completed an about-face 180 degree rotation. The unborn heart rate rapidly returns to its normal 130-140 beats per minute. I can breathe.

"That's enough." I stand, releasing Myesha's abdomen while sliding my right arm out from between her legs. Myesha regains her two-legged human appearance, losing the alien middle limb of my elbow extending from her vagina.

Donda and I glance at one another, with unspoken relief as the fetal heart rate returns to normal. "Your baby wonders 'What's happening?'" I joke, making light of our quickly resolved concern.

"Is he OK?" Myesha asks, eyeing the bedside monitor.

"He recovered. He's a strong little guy, just like his mamma. Let's see your next push."

With her next push Myesha's pink vagina quickly spreads open as we expect for a fourth baby, revealing a growing mass of wet black hair descending in the ideal position. The unborn scalp visibly twists side to side, navigating life's longest six-inch journey. I quickly pull on another pair of sterile gloves. Donda calls the pediatric nurse to come for a birth.

Myesha's dark folds bloom like a black rose under time lapse photography. The wedge of dark wetness between smooth vaginal lips follows seconds later by a crown of wet black curls. Supporting Myesha's perineum with my left hand, the baby's head and shoulders with my right, a floppy silent baby boy surrenders to life. Myesha extends her arms, drawing the wet purple baby to her breast. Frank briefly glances down at the wet newborn.

Sally, the pediatric nurse, steps to Myesha's bedside. She anticipates a stunned baby because such a rapid change of environment can surprise the most hardy of newborns. A gurgle erupts from tiny swollen purple lips. Sally vigorously massages the limp baby, her green rubber bulb suctions fluid from tiny mouth and nostrils. She holds an oxygen mask to his face.

Myesha encourages, "Come on, little man! You're here," bouncing her son in her arms.

His obligatory task completed, Frank drops Myesha's leg and turns away. He plops upon the green leather sofa to begin tapping his Blackberry phone's keypad.

After a long 30 seconds, Myesha's little man emits his first cry.

"He's beautiful," Myesha coos. Then looking up she asks, "Will you put ointment in his eyes now?" referring to antibiotics to prevent gonorrhea from infecting his eyes.

"In a few minutes," Sally reassures her. "He'll be OK."

Despite encouragement, Myesha refuses to breastfeed. "I can't breastfeed. I have to return to work soon. It's too hard when I leak milk." She gracefully pulls long blond braids behind ebony shoulders. Exaggerated plastic eyelashes surround her dark eyes as they lock with mine as if to emphasize her subtext.

"I understand." I nod. "But get some good contraception from the clinic before you return to work!"

Myesha laughs, "No kidding!"

"And remember raincoats to block those pesky critters!" I use street slang to reference condoms.

Myesha rolls her eyes and laughs, acknowledging my words while cradling the son in her arms. One acrylic green fingernail strokes a pudgy cheek, then traces tiny puckered lips in a bubble of mother-love.

ERIC HUCKE

Flying the Hump

1.

The Brahmaputra Valley
               sweltered in the Monsoon
While we watched
               for planes returning
Over the treacherous
               snow capped Himalayas.
In his eighties
               retired from teaching
Children grown up
               wife gone crazy
Wes tells me over
               and over again
How it was
               forecasting weather
For the China-Burma airlift.
"If we got it wrong
               they didn't come back."

2.

Saturday morning in the ICU
                nurses work feverishly.
"It's a massive coronary,
                he's not going to make it,"
The doctor tells me.

Toward noon
                Wes bolts upright
Arms outstretched
                eyes staring into the distance
Then falls back.

Was it his lost comrades
                he saw at last
I wondered
                or the far mountains
Of Himavant
                Hindu god of snow?

During WWII close to 600 planes were lost flying the China-Burma
"Hump" and 1659 airmen were reported killed or missing.
                                        - US Air force report

Everybody Gets Something

At our first class reunion
        everyone got drunk.
By the tenth we all thought
        we were hot stuff.
Obnoxious would be
        a better word for it.
But after thirty years
        things had changed.
My wife was chronically ill
        and I had left the ministry,
Mike was a recovering alcoholic,
        Dick died in a car accident,
Steve had open heart surgery,
        Barbara was a cancer survivor,
Nancy died of scleroderma,
        Sheila's daughter was killed in an accident,
Marvel's son committed suicide,
        and so on,
           and so on.
All, except for Darrell.

Somehow, Darrell had married
        the pretty girl,
Had a great job,
        and life was good.
Naturally, Darrell thought
        pretty highly of himself.
Let's face it, he had become
        a real pain in the ass.
Then, came the thirty-fifth.

By this time
        my marriage had ended
And I was not looking forward
        to meeting Darrell.

Arriving early at the cocktail party
        I spotted him
Standing over in the corner
        all alone
Looking down
        at his shoe tops.
Looking down at his shoe tops?
        This can't be!
Eventually I worked
        my way over.
"How's it going, Darrell?"
        "Not so good,
I lost my job."
        Well, I thought,
Join the club.
        Join the human race!
Next year is our fiftieth.
        I'm looking forward
To seeing Darrell
        along with everyone else.
Only this time
        we will all be glad
Just to be alive.

A Reprieve

Sitting hunched
        in her worn bathrobe
Her sunken death row eyes
        watch me coldly.
"No job
        no insurance
           no place to live
And my mother's
        not well either.
So, I've come home
        to die."
Shortly after my visit
        Merry played her final card.
Refusing more chemo
        her weight returned
Her hair grew out
        her eyes brightened.
And by Easter
        death's dark angel
Seemed somehow
        to have passed her over.
In summer Merry grew stronger
        came to church
Read scriptures on Sunday
        joined the book club.
We hoped for the best.
        "I do have cancer."
She reminded us politely.

Yet, by Christmas
        Merry still seemed well.
But as every Minnesotan knows
        "there's no cheating winter."

After the holidays
>> the lakes froze over
>>> snow fell

And Merry was back
>> in the hospital.

The malignancy
>> now in her lungs.

"I don't want you to die, Merry."
>> I told her.

Nodding her head
>> she smiled weakly.

Easter came early that year
>> with no sign of spring.

At her funeral
>> we passed out balloons

And sang the ancient Irish prayer
>> "Be Thou My Vision."

It had been a good year
>> all around.

Elegy for Merry Coleman, 1955-2002

JOHN FOX

Letting The Light In
(And Creative Ways to Spread It Around)

> *This little light of mine, I'm going to let it shine*
> *This little light of mine, I'm going to let it shine*
> *This little light of mine, I'm going to let it shine*
> *Let it shine, Let it shine, Let it shine.*
>
> Harry Dixon Loes

There is something in and to this song by Harry Dixon Loes, a song comprised of about twelve words total, that says something that is far more than the sum of its parts. This sweet song became a Civil Rights anthem in the 50's and 60's, and was sung by Odetta with the Boys' Choir on *The Late Show with David Letterman* on September 17, 2001, which was the first show after Letterman resumed broadcasting following the events of 9/11. (I urge my reader to look at this very moving recording of Odetta. You can Google it at: *Odetta Letterman 9/11 You Tube*—and you will find it.)

You could, like I have just done, like Odetta and Harlem Boys Choir on Letterman, sing this song and I think you could sing it pretty easily.

Letting your light shine. You could just let it happen, this song, even what it says, *let it happen.* You could. And in a way, considering your true origin, you already do.

We can take our time though. I'd like to explore with you those two words *"let it."* I think the whole song revolves around and is rooted in the fertile ground of those two simple words, *"let it."* If the words *"let it"* were a living planet, they are, like a living planet, what makes possible both the "mine" and the "shining" possible.

And also, as the song gets going, something flies free like a bird, like a soul, flies free from the branch of those words where the "mine" or at least the "mine" alone may disappear, in the "let it shine." There may be in those words an impulse of flight towards not only joining but Oneness. You know, birds of a feather.

These are not complicated and intellectual words: "let it." They are straightforward. They suggest, in a way, the simplest kind of action required. The Free Online Dictionary has these things to say about the words let, letting, and lets:

let[1]

v. **let, let·ting, lets**

v.tr.

1. To give permission or opportunity to; allow:
2. To cause to; make:
4. To permit to enter, proceed, or depart:
5. To release from or as if from confinement:

All of these definitional facets of the words let and letting and let are worth exploring. And I think they all relate to what this song is saying to us. In the walking from Selma to Montgomery in the Civil Rights movement, in the laying down of lives, that song was all about a release from cultural chains. As a way to lift their spirits beyond that confinement it was sung in prison by children and by adults.

I'm particularly caught, however, by the 2nd definition offered for "letting": to "cause to" or "make." There is something in this "making" that is very close to or is identical to the roots, the origins of the word "poetry."

The Greek word for poetry is *"poesis"* and it means literally *"to make."* And even more specifically is connected to the Greek word *poiein*, or creation. Poesis, like the word *let,* is the act of making. Poesis means to produce something specific. Create it. I'm following a trail here with the word "let," which leads to the words cause or make, which leads to the words poesis and creation.

Galway Kinnell describes poetry as an "artifact," a making of "something physical out of words." Carl Sagan, astronomer, astrophysicist, and cosmologist, said in the breathtaking series *Cosmos*, "The beauty of a living thing is not the atoms that go into it but the way those atoms are put together."

Both poet Kinnell and astronomer Sagan are saying that the creation of beauty involves *making*—whether it is making/composing something physical out of words, or of atoms.

When we watch Odetta call forth from deep within herself the word "Let" you could see it in her posture as she stepped and we witness the radiant smiles of the Harlem Boys' Choir singing literally let it shine—and right after September 11, 2011, we see how Henry Dixon Loes' gospel and those who are made of atoms to sing it beautifully, we get a hint of what poet and astronomer mean.

But I want to get back to those simple words *let it shine* …

As I wrote this essay, I had this stirring sense in me, a stirring sense about all these words, these threads of definitions, these root-place of words, of something more than the sum of its parts. This ground I was on. There was some ancient feeling in me that this word "let" may have happened very, very early on (at least within some western tradition or reality); if I am talking about making things, of creation, *letting* is essential and important.

I'm no biblical scholar, yet I am a guy who follows trails and especially trails when it comes to the word. I'm often looking for the trailhead of words. Since it's *creating* I am speaking about, I thought of beginnings, or another word, for beginning … genesis … which means *coming into being*. Another creation word! A creation word that comes via Old English: via Latin from Greek; related to the Greek *gignesthai* to be born.

I was even open to touching in with *"the"* in quotes and italics, in the

Beginning as in capital B. Following a hunch that there maybe something BIG about this word "let." I tell you the truth, I was seeing that through a glass darkly. It was a hunch not a knowing for sure. So I looked.

Sometimes, even if one isn't schooled or even if, I'll say it this way—if I don't remember what I learned in confirmation class from Mrs. Steedman at the Church of the Saviour in Cleveland Heights OH, one can still hit the nail on the head!

The first chapter of Genesis, verse 3 says that, "LET" is the first word spoken by God or the Spirit. God was, apparently, pretty darn quiet and hovering around for those first two verses. But then, whoa, watch out ...

Let there be light ... and so it goes on—*let there be water, vegetation, stars, creatures* ... all of these immense and beautiful realities are preceded by the word *let.* I think to myself: This isn't even an actual word, is it? *Let* must be a poor echo of some vivid silence that is waking up right in front of us, or it is some subtle vibration that suddenly opens the heart, this letting.

Genesis, in this sense, is the original invocation of letting.

I'm just getting warmed up. Although I was excited by this connection to the word "let" in that first chapter of, in the very first verses, of Genesis, and while I am a true believer in metaphor, you can trust me that I'm not a Bible-thumper. So please don't stop reading just yet. Not yet. Let me have a chance.

> "That the sky is brighter than the earth means little unless the earth itself is appreciated and enjoyed. Its beauty loved gives the right to aspire to the radiance of the sunrise and sunset."
>
> - Helen Keller, from *My Religion,* 1927

So what would it be like if we let it, could we simply practice letting, that is, to allow ourselves, to permit ourselves to enter, to release from confinement, what if we were to give permission for that? These words indicate a way of being—allow, permit, enter, release—all are gathered around letting. But how can we really get there?

Helen Keller invites us to love the earth as a preliminary step to identify more deeply—aspire to—that is, connect within ourselves with light, the sunrise and sunset. Jane Kenyon invites us with the lines:

> Let the light of late afternoon
> shine through chinks in the barn, moving
> up the bales as the sun moves down.

These first images are not of evening or night but rather the slanting sunlight late in the day. Not only that but at this particular time of day, as this light slants and nears the horizon, it flares through little spaces between barn boards. Those "chinks" make for a kind of distilling down and fanning out of light that also lets shadow in and can simultaneously focus and heighten sunlight's brightness. She does not say this but I see those pale bales of hay turn golden, at least for a moment, until the sun moves down entirely.

As a poet she helps me, she helps us, *to let this happen.* We need ways to learn a practice of letting—letting go, letting in, maybe at times, yes, letting loose, and without doubt, to let it be.

"Let Evening Come" shows us what occurs in the rural evening. Kenyon, who died from melanoma in 1994, way too early in her mid 40s, was a long-time resident of New Hampshire. She lived there with her husband, the poet Donald Hall. Her images are often of this rural place.

In a lovely way, all the things in her poem are illumined softly by the coming on of evening. That's a paradox of poetry, how something can come alive and vivid even as we start to see less.

The word "let" is used to invoke this atmosphere—invoke it not as stern demand but as a call, an appeal for space. We see and recognize and make space for each unique and sacred thing. In this poem, evening is in close touch with many things: dew, the moon, the cricket, the fox, the hoe, the scoop.

What makes this letting in the light, this letting go at evening time, this letting there be more space ... why and what is it so difficult about this for us humans?

We need to find ways to let evening come. Kenyon's words bring us to that edge ...

Words, that can so often fail us like so many wet matches, also have the potential to light on fire –to light my life, light up the life of others. And I love it when words can make—as in the word poesis—can make a connection with that which is at the beginning, something like stars:

There Is An Origin

For each true poem born there is an origin:
Blessed ignorance of words that turn
To splendid fire, as stars in space will yearn
To find on earth their up stretched twin

- John Fox

But this poem is not really, at its heart, about making poems. The poem is a metaphor for our capacity as human beings to create like stars. It is about living a life that can catch fire, that in doing so, like those stars, like our lives, we let our unique light shine.

It's light, first and last, that calls me. But are you and I to live this kind of life when there are so many other necessities and demands? I think we need to keep asking ourselves: what am I here for?

Carl Sagan said in the series Cosmos: "We are a way for the universe to know itself. Some part of our being knows this is where we came from. We long to return. And we can, because the cosmos is also within us. We're made of star-stuff." Chris Impey, professor of astronomy at the University of Arizona, told Life's Little Mysteries: "Because humans and every other animal—as well as most of the matter on Earth—contain these elements [carbon, nitrogen and oxygen atoms], we are literally made of star stuff ... All organic matter containing carbon was produced originally in stars."

Again, I've thought about this a lot. Not just in an abstract scientific way regarding carbon, which is amazing, or simply the sheer fact & wonder of it, sort of letting fact and wonder dance together full tilt, but how it is true in the midst of our suffering and the way living this life does its deep work on us, because we are in some relationship to life itself, that the capacity to shine can come about:

When Jewels Sing

Radiance results from earth's pressure,
life working on us with each moment's precision
into clear cut uniqueness.
A community of precious human beings
with origins primitive and wild as diamonds,
faceted by skilled and invisible hands that turn us
upon a wheel dusted with God's bright dark silence,
we become men and women joined to walk
swarthy, holy, original and transparent.
Catching first light of day upon ourselves,
our voices sing of truth and loveliness,
in response to vows first sung to us by stars.

- John Fox

This light that we let in might be not so far away in our everyday life. We may not always need or be drawn to such mystical perspectives. The poet Charles Olson said "I have had to learn the simplest things last, and that has made for difficulty." This letting in of the light might be apparent right in your home.

I lead ongoing poetry circles in the Bay Area, and a woman attending one of those circles is going through a major transition in her life. Carol has stripped things down in her home, which was the home of her mother, in order to let in more light, so she can see more of what is right there.

Window Treatments

Light pours through
bare windows once
draped in coral
peau de soie swags.

Sunlight warms the
new maple floor,

shines on the walnut
dining room table
once kept in the dark.

So it will last. And it has.
        Lasted.

Now it stands bare
in bright morning light
revealing its grain.

- Carol Howard-Wooton

RUTH SAXEY-REESE

blue hour
it was the rabbit hour
the jackrabbit
passed my window
obedient

I followed
down the steps
across the street
up the draw

I found
it was also
the dove hour
the vole hour
the pine hour
the gnat hour

turning home
the creek
made it
the buck hour

beneath my shawl
I became
the blue hour
fixed
as blue is

the buck
ticked ahead
on asphalt

then doubled back
keeping
the hour blue

the hour
swept
wet eyes

counted
velvet tines

the buck and the hour
breathed

veni, columba
come down, dove
rewrite
my white-feather birth

come down
I will recite
my father, a talon
my mother, the breeze

myself
a moon sliver
nearly consumed
first breath
like drowning

come down
mirror milk

come down
concede
the sainted space
between heart and voice

Dear Dr. Haynes,

During one of my recent surgeries, some clown must have switched out
      my tongue.
Preoccupied with yet more stitches, I didn't really notice it

fusing to the back of my mouth, the way it pressed my teeth
and gagged me when I swallowed pills,

but then it learned to unhook itself and escape at night.
Slobbering on all my notebooks wasn't so bad;

smacking the dogs down the hall and
bitch-slapping my daughter went too far.

When it tried to lick a priest, I cut it out and threw it into the street—
it hopped back in, flooding my mouth with warm salt.

I've tried biting bits off while I'm chewing a steak.
I've tried to swallow it whole, but only choked and passed out.

Now it's slowly stitching my mouth shut from the inside.
Soon I will be mute.
Don't tell me it's not in the literature.

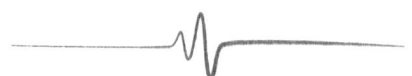

SARAH PARIS

Summer Breeze

What if I understood what one bird calls the other
or what the doe thinks, standing in my path—
in *her* path—surely, deer don't deal in thoughts.
Her eyes observe me out of fleck-white corners.

I settle down into a likeness of the statue
of Virgin Mary, miming purity of mind,
erasing wayward thoughts to clear
a space that lets the moment be.

If I can keep a virgin mind, will emptiness
become the cloak that makes me undetectable
and shields us both from fear? The doe
sets one foot forward, then another. Slow-motion
dance that stops at a perceived obstruction.
She settles down to graze.

Is it important that she step across
the threshold of imagined grace? Or isn't it enough
that she is here. And breathes, along with me
(and with the birds) the same, warm summer breeze.

Must I Show It To Her?

Of all of them, it had to be *your* door
propped open, catching the attention of
the visiting reporter and his camera.
You had gone to take a shower.

No, the photo doesn't show how small
it really is. But you told me once you easily
can put your hands flat up against
the ceiling, even touch both walls at once.

Everything is tidy. We both know she'll like that.
All your books, your typewriter, each covered
with the silky cloths she sent you. I won't
tell her of the dust that permeates the air.

Above all, I will not focus her attention
to the vent low in the wall, just large enough
for one small, agile rat to squeeze through
(or make lots of noise while trying.)

She won't like the vintage pin-ups.
She will wonder why you didn't hang
her photo on the wall above your desk.

I'll explain to her about the random
searches when they rip off everything.
And you couldn't bear to see her face torn.

I will also have to mention that the "desk"
is just a metal bunk, covered with your stuff.
You sleep on the floor, so if you have
a seizure, you won't fall and crack your head.

At this point, she'll spot the mattress,
rolled up, standing in the corner, just two
inches thick. Two thin blankets,
one small plastic pillow.

That's when she will start to cry, as it hits her:
More than thirty years you've been locked up here.
How could any human bear it?

So I'm asking you again: Are you really sure
you want to show this photograph to her?

Ask Her Why She Drinks

A searing look, an eyebrow full of *what the fuck?*
Don't move your gaze; wait 'til she turns away,
juts out her chin. *Do I look drunk to you?*

Note very calmly: "That was your third shot."
So what? You wanna dance? Try me, see if I can't
still turn hot circles 'round your skinny butt!

Don't take her dare. Keep watch, while her eyes wander
across the stained glass window at the bar's front end.
Hey, it's Tequila, or it's Valium …

Is she in pain? *Sure, darlin', everyone is hurtin'.*
This is a blues bar, Jeezus—we're all dying
to thrust a knife into our aching hearts, but meanwhile—

Huck! The bartender brings her another shot. *A toast!*
"To what?" *Whose story do you want to hear, my friend?*
What myth in my voluminous biography would satisfy?

Let's see: A lonely childhood? (Yeah, what else is new.)
The absent father? Sure. Perhaps some incest? Or a little rape, maybe …
or was it really? We all forget, we all play smoke and mirrors.

A Cheshire cat grin. *But—what if I told you that my life is happy?*
The perfect job, a sweet and loving husband? If I had everything
a woman might desire, who is to blame? My wicked genes?

She leans in closer. *Don't you know that deep down we're all yearning*
to kill what we can't—

—stops herself, breaks into laughter.
Hell, what a joke! Look who I am talking to!

FRAN DORF

Plastic Man

Chapter One of a memoir entitled:
How I Lost My Bellybutton,
And Other Naked Survival Stories

Survival Tip #1: When you are required to make a decision, medical or otherwise, that could have truly grave consequences, no matter how old you are, how much you've been through in your life, how much you think you've learned, or how heated a rush you're in to make your decision and get on with it, always remember to treat yourself kindly and with care, do your homework, and take your sweet time.

"So let's see what you got."

The interview part was now over, and Plastic Man rose behind the consultation room desk. There was a cool hush to the place and little in these glam surroundings to indicate I was even in a doctor's office with a human doctor. If the doctor had any kids there were no photos of them here, although several large abstract oil paintings dominated the huge, crowded waiting room, along with hundreds of exotic orchids in large, Zen-contoured vases. The whole office suite, in fact, was a highly styled, ultra-modern showplace, spare and posh and designed to befit a successful Manhattan plastic surgeon. It was also no doubt intended to be a soothing space, its aggressively non-medical aesthetic trying hard to banish any bothersome concern that plastic surgery, after all, is a medical procedure that might be associated with real pain and suffering.

Plastic Man himself, the third plastic surgeon I'd seen since being diagnosed with breast cancer, was in his forties, his face pleasant if a little bland. He had answered my list of questions not so differently than the other two plastic surgeons I'd consulted.

But you'd think this pioneer in his field and professor at the distinguished medical school who came with the mile-long resume and the crowded waiting room would have had a little respect. (Not to mention better grammar.) Or at least shown me some sympathy. I had cancer.

No respect here, let alone sympathy. Plastic Man wanted to see "what I got," by which he meant my fifty-something breasts and belly.

And did I really hate that belly so much that I was contemplating getting rid of it along with my breast via a mastectomy and a complicated, bizarre surgical operation known as a TRAM flap reconstruction? The truth is, I had already decided I probably was. The only question was which plastic surgeon I would pick to do it.

I was so shocked that even if I'd pried my mouth open with pliers my brain couldn't have formed a response, not even a smart-ass one, like maybe, "You want to see what I got? Why don't you show me what *you* got?"

Now you, the reader, might legitimately ask why I hadn't brought my husband of thirty-five years to this appointment. The answer is, I just thought I'd give him a pass on this one, because he'd dutifully accompanied me to the last five: Breast Surgeons #1 through #3 and Plastic Surgeons #1 and #2. I've always wondered what would have happened if Bob had been in the room that day. Maybe he would have ushered me out the door. Maybe, being a person who's dealt with plenty of dreadful medical experiences of his own and who often deals with things through humor, he would have come up with his own smart-ass rejoinder.

I asked Bob about it this morning. We were sitting at the kitchen table, and my husband, who's gone nearly nearly gray and whose face has gone from handsome to craggy-handsome, said: "I probably wouldn't have said anything, because I likely would have been intimidated." Which of course just shows you the effect doctors can have on mere mortals. Bob, who's survived two bouts with cancer and a brain tumor, who started and ran two big companies, and who at sixty is as strong as an ox, works like a thirty-year-old, and can go 100 miles on a bicycle practically without breaking a sweat—as opposed to me who would drop dead at the five-mile marker—*intimidated*?

On the other hand, how do you ever know what *would* have happened? Especially since you can bet your boopie that Plastic Man wouldn't have asked to see "what I got" if my husband were there. Or would he?

And just so the reader knows, I try not to dwell on these kinds of questions very often as a general rule, because what's the point? Which brings us to:

Survival Tip #2: Do not cry too much over spilt milk.

And:

Survival Tip #3: Bring your husband, your partner, or someone who cares about you to all appointments with physicians when the diagnosis is bad, and especially when it involves making an important decision, no matter how competent or emotionally together you think you are. You need an advocate.

As for me, I desperately needed an advocate that morning because I had in effect emotionally detached myself from the enormous and essential task before me, the task that befalls most American woman diagnosed with breast cancer. You have not one but three doctors to pick, often in great haste while terrified: the breast surgeon, the plastic surgeon (if you choose to have one), and the oncologist. Picking three doctors you like who all happen to work or have privileges in the same hospital isn't easy, even if you're playing with a relatively full deck. I wasn't.

Why? Well, I might as well explain right here. My diagnosis had come just six weeks before my daughter's wedding. The invitations were already out, we had a hundred and sixty people coming, and all I could think of all summer was how this whole surprise cancer thing felt like some sort of Jobian plot against me and my family—God was ONCE AGAIN going to prevent me from going into an event of celebration of Rachel (and her wonderful husband to be) with a full, undistracted heart. I once spent about two years in a similar state of paranoid depression and self-flagellation, wondering why God was picking on me, and sometimes such states lie dormant in the bones and cells only to reemerge when triggered by another stress-producing event.

You see, fourteen years before my breast cancer diagnosis I lost a child, my three-year-old son, Michael. I'll get to that later in this memoir but for now I'll just lay out the weird coincidence that so disturbed me that breast cancer/wedding summer. At the time my son became ill, my own personal Pearl Harbor Day, December 7, 1993, my daughter was already scheduled to have her Bat Mitzvah, the celebration that occurs when a Jewish daughter turns thirteen. Rachel's birthday is in February, and we'd scheduled the Bat Mitzvah for March and booked a party room for the bash we'd planned to follow her Torah reading in the synagogue. But *our son was dying*, and we couldn't very well have a celebration of life in the midst of death, and so we postponed the Bat Mitsvah—indefinitely. When we finally had it a year later it was like inviting everyone we knew to a party and showing up naked, wearing nothing but our grief.

Up against yet another catastrophe in the face of celebration, I think I may have dissociated. Telling myself it was only DCIS, ductal carcinoma in situ, sort of breast cancer lite, I went on the assumption that I could and would emerge from it essentially unscathed and concentrated on wedding details. The result was my dissociation from the threat to my life, from the importance of making the right decisions about the threat, and especially from connection between the decisions I made and the outcome.

Now the TRAM flap is one of the options you're given when you can't get by with just a lumpectomy and radiation—your cancer *in situ* has shown up in two quadrants of your left breast, making it impossible to get a "cosmetically acceptable" result with a lumpectomy, so you have to get the whole *megillah*—mastectomy. On the bright side, with the whole *megillah* you probably don't have to have radiation *or* chemotherapy. Yeah!

Once you accept that a lumpectomy won't do it and mastectomy is your only option, you can consider whether to have them take both breasts, the right one too as a preventative measure, and then you can:

A) replace the breast (or breasts) with nothing

B) replace the breast (or breasts) with saline or silicone implants, or

C) replace the breast (or breasts) with flesh from somewhere else on the body—namely the buttocks (known to my foremothers and fathers as a *tuches*), back, or belly.

The belly replacement, option C, is called the TRAM flap, and you might say this is the only time in life in which having belly fat is a good thing. Think about it.

But wasn't this tempting fate, when I'd already had three other operations in the same area in my life, a ruptured ovarian cyst at twenty, a hysterectomy at forty-eight, and an intestinal blockage at fifty from adhesions caused by scar tissue from the previous two operations?

I asked all three plastic surgeons, including Plastic Man, this question. All three said three previous operations didn't matter, I'd be fine. Not one mentioned the possibility of complications. Maybe that word is left out of plastic surgeon training.

Plastic Man made one concession: "We'll do a pedicled TRAM if the blood supply isn't adequate."

None of the other surgeons had mentioned this.

"What's that?"

"We push the tissue under the skin from the belly into the breast."

"As opposed to what?" It was actually the first time a doctor had offered a physical description of the TRAM. I never even seriously researched the procedure. I was oblivious to the fact that having such a complicated operation increased rather than decreased the threat to my life, which I was also oblivious to. I was stuck in the notion that my chances of something going wrong were no better or worse than anyone else's, no matter what I did, that as Rabbi Kushner tells us, bad things happen to good people all the time—after all, a really bad thing, the worst thing, had already happened to me.

"Microsurgery." His manner was as neutral as tea. "Disconnecting and reconnecting the tissue."

Disconnecting and reconnecting tissue? Pushing tissue from belly to breast? Who was I—Dr. Frankenstein's daughter? Was I REALLY contemplating doing this? Grow-old-with-dignity, anti-plastic-surgery *me*? What about my principles? What about wanting to go serenely and happily into my dotage with my experience, wisdom, and goodness etched on my body and face? What about my belief that these bodies are only the shells of us, and that as we age we should care less about our shells and more about our hearts? For God's sake, the Greeks knew that, and I know it too, even if our culture has turned this truth on its head by worshipping youth and beauty as the highest ideal rather than goodness and wisdom, which only come with age and experience, two commodities of which at the age of 57 I have plenty.

Well, maybe a breast cancer diagnosis meant all bets were off when it came to principles, and while I was already under I might as well get the equivalent of a tummy tuck with my mastectomy, as in I'll have bacon with my eggs, make lemonade out of my lemons. Except that I hate eggs, which along with caviar fall into my inedible category, unborn beings, and I have never been a "lemonade out of lemons" kind of person. It seems to me that Jews, religiously observant or otherwise (I belong to the latter category), are generally not lemonade out of lemons kind of people (Well, except in the sense that we keep *surviving*, no matter what.) We look under the glass rather than in it. In previous generations, we whispered the names of diseases. We don't ski. Except I do ski. But hey, I can explain.

Thirty-five years ago I married a Jew named Bob Dorf who *is* a lemonade kind of person, a very persuasive lemonade kind of person, and he insisted I ski along with him. As the reader will learn, I come from a stunningly non-lemonade (not to mention non-skiing) family, and I must have secretly (or perhaps unknowingly) wanted or needed to hook up with a lemonade kind of person, because I can't figure out any other reason why I make a thirty-three-year habit out of an activity in which the basic idea is that you strap two three-inch-wide boards on your feet and head downhill on the treacherous ice of very steep mountains, freezing your tootsies off and hoping to survive. Jews do not do this. Jews eat. Jews call their travel agents and book guilt trips. Jews kvetch. Jews make jokes. I may not be much of a Jew, and my mother was a committed atheist, but I know how to eat, kvetch, and make jokes. It's in the molecules.

Plastic Man waved a hand at the cabinets along the wall, said, "There's a gown in there. I'll be back," and was nearly out the opaque white glass door. I did have one last question.

"Why'd you become a plastic surgeon?"

He stopped and stared at me for a moment, shrugged, said, "That's a long story," and opened the door. And then he was gone.

My face flushed. Why'd I ask him that stupid question, anyway? Did I think I could trip him up? Hope he'd say he thought of plastic surgery as human art? Confirm he was only in it for the money, had a warped concept of beauty, once fell in love with a girl with a big nose who dumped him? I have no idea, but I know his answer left me embarrassed for having asked.

Survival Tip #4: If during the interview process a doctor refuses to answer your questions, dismisses your concerns in any way, or puts you down, pay attention and head for the hills before it's too late.

I pulled off my shirt, my bra. At this point I was already a pro at this, well acquainted with the guiding principle of the breast cancer experience, that you're simply going to have to bare your breasts to everyone who wants to see them. I looked down at mine. The left one. The right one. The left one would soon be gone. I would never see it gone, though, never have to be faced with some half woman, half boy, deformed version of myself, because when I woke up after the surgery I'd already have the new breast. The thought of this new breast contributed to my fantasy that I would emerge from all of this not so different from before.

Actually better, since the plastic surgeon would put on the nipple during a second operation and fix the other breast to match the new, smaller one. Though my husband seemed happy enough with the pair I had now, I didn't particularly like them. I had loved breast-feeding my daughter, but as far as I was concerned they were too big. Which was fine when I was twenty, though their size made them a source of male attention I was less capable of coping with than I'd have admitted. Now, it was a different story.

I started to pull off my capri pants off but they got stuck on the ridiculous shoes I was wearing. Kitten-heeled sandals. It was summer and boiling hot outside these cool confines—global warming, of course. I pulled the pants back up, sat down in the chair. I noticed my hands were shaking and it took me a few moments to get the buckle undone.

The thing is, I'm not really a plastic surgery kind of gal. In fact, I'm so disgusted by all the plastic surgery in this misogynous culture that I once wrote a short story in which all the plastic surgeons all over the United States suddenly begin to turn into warthogs. (Hey, if metamorphosis is good enough for Kafka, it's good enough for me.)

Turning plastic surgeons into warthogs seemed to me at the time I wrote the story like perfect payback. Here, after all, is a burgeoning industry of highly trained salesmen who in the name of some impossible ideal keep turning out these stretched-scary women, who seem to feel empowered rather than demeaned by sporting faces so inert they look as if pod-born space aliens have taken up residence. What could be more appropriate than to turn every last plastic man (and/or woman) into a warthog? I've come across warthogs in the sub-Saharan bush and the warthog, with the possible exception of the manatee and Donald Trump, is the ugliest creature I've ever seen.

Consider the squat wrinkled body of the warthog, the frizzled Mohawk of a mane; the irregularly formed face with its multitude of fleshy protuberances, the long piggy proboscis, the drooping eyes, oddly placed back near the crown of the warthog head and its stump of a neck. And do not forget the four tusks that in addition to the warts protrude alarmingly from the warthog face, two of which are short stumpy affairs and two of which are long and curl back in on themselves. Imagine what happens when all the plastic surgeons in America come down with a mysterious, untreatable condition that turns them into *that*. I'll tell you what happens. They go grunting off into oblivion, confined to internment camps where they roll around in the mud to their little warthog hearts' content, thereby leaving women no choice but to stop trying to fix themselves, since they're fine as they are.

Survival Tip #5: An oldie but a goodie. Be who you are. If you don't know who you are, find out.

I just loved that warthog tale, even though no one wanted to publish it. But wasn't I in karmic terms tempting fate by choosing the most aggressive, invasive plastic surgery option available to me? Maybe I should leave well enough alone and spit into the air three times (*tst, tst, tst*) like my Grandma Belle might have.

The truth is, I decided maybe it was okay to dispense with consistency of thought regarding plastic surgery when you had breast cancer anyway, and with all the pressure I was feeling to schedule this surgery and get to the wedding, I never even seriously considered the less invasive implant operation. I certainly never considered the option of letting the surgeon cut off the breast and walking around with one breast for the rest of my life, as my Grandma Belle or even my mother would have done. (Grandma would have done this partly because no alternative would have been available to her, and my God, would it have compromised her vertical stability, given the size, weight, and mass of her breasts.)

I focused on the idea of doing what all the surgeons, including this one, said would feel most natural. Which makes sense, since you'd have to figure even transplanted flesh would feel more natural and soft than an implant made in a factory. And I was a natural gal. Hadn't I worn a rawhide headband, hung out stoned at rock festivals, protested Vietnam? Hey, I was a natural teenage earth mother when Plastic Man was about seven.

He was knocking on the door. Seemed quick. I had laid my clothing across the chair in the corner, bra hidden under my pants. (I always do this with doctors in examining rooms, do you?)

"Come in."

In he came and I was standing there like a frightened twelve-year-old and he silently walked over and opened the green gown.

Now reader, there was another clue. The other male plastic surgeon I'd seen examined me in an examining room, with a nurse present. Plastic Man and I were still in the consulting room. But maybe the rules in Manhattan were different.

Anyway, it didn't matter. Plastic Man had my left breast in his hands, the one with the cancer, and he was silently moving it this way, that way.

I closed my eyes. He was a bit rough, and somehow it reminded me of my Grandma Belle making her strudel. She'd slap down a hunk of dough about the same size as my breast on the kitchen table, then she'd knead it and slap it and knead it and slap it. Plastic Man wasn't doing any slapping, but there was definitely some kneading involved. And I'm thinking: What a weird profession.

But I could do this. I was going to get through this.

Now he had the other breast in his hand, and he was handling it the same way. And I was wondering why, when you've suffered through child loss, you didn't get a pass on cancer.

Survival Tip #6: Sorry, kid, life doesn't work that way.

He had moved down to my belly now, the part of my body that had changed so much when I had my daughter, the part I truly hated. Okay, so he was a little rough. But if this is how he worked, so be it. He was one of the top doctors in the field. He was Plastic Man.

But what about sympathy? Maybe I should try to get his by telling him everything I'd been through in my life, including the worst of the worst. Damn. I was never going to get through this if I kept letting myself go there. I had learned long ago, mostly, to compartmentalize, to control when I would let myself think about my son, since it's your only choice as a bereaved mother. Unfortunately this coping tool wasn't working very well that morning, not well at all.

And what would Plastic Man in his designer offices care anyway that my life was starting to sound like the winning sob story on *Queen for a Day*— the original reality show, back in the 1950's. A real gem. On *Queen for a Day*, a succession of dowdy middle-aged female contestants appeared on stage and told hard luck stories *(Mother has cancer, husband lost job; house burned down, child needs wheelchair)*. The audience judged the pathos of each contestant's story via the "applause meter," then the winner who got the loudest applause was draped in a robe and crown and given a washing machine and a night on the town.

Okay, stop. I was in this doctor's office because I was trying to pick the plastic surgeon. You didn't pick a surgeon on whether you liked him or not, or whether he liked you, offered you a scintilla or a barge load of respect, felt sorry for you or didn't. A thirty-year string of medical issues meant I'd had way more than my share of experience with doctors, and I'd run into the ones who exhibit compassion about as often as ones who didn't. My son's first neurologist may as well have been a robot, for example, although the physician in charge of the pediatric ward at the long term care hospital where Michael finally landed was gentle, and compassionate, and human, and altogether remarkable, thank God. But if I could handle Dr. Robot (well, I didn't handle him *that* well considering that I did a number on my stand-in for him in my novel, Saving Elijah), I could handle Plastic Man. All that mattered, I told myself, was surgical skill. He had a great reputation on that score.

And now Plastic Man disappeared again without another word while

I stood there clutching the shreds of my dignity, trying not to cry. He reappeared with a Polaroid camera and started shooting pictures of my naked torso. After that he sent me into another room where there was a technician with a machine that takes three-dimensional pictures of the breasts and has something to do with getting the breast volume right for matching one to the other. This seemed impressive, of course. You certainly don't want one breast substantially different from the other.

All these photos plus the humiliation of standing there naked and dissociated and defenseless and not playing with a full deck plus the terror of having breast cancer in the first place called for distracting interior jokes: Could Plastic Man be planning to blackmail me? Would I see all these pictures on the Internet with a flashing nametag the next time I went online?

Then my only option would be to post a rebuttal comment.

REBUTTAL COMMENT

Believe it or not, the middle-aged woman you see here was once offered several thousand dollars to pose for a famous men's magazine. She was such a screwy adolescent, and so needy, that she actually considered it for a minute. On the other hand, if she'd taken the money she'd have it as proof that she once had breasts that weren't starting to point to her bellybutton. Of course, before all this is over she'll have two perky breasts that stand at attention as if they were nineteen again, and she won't even have a bellybutton. Does that mean she will be unborn?

"So," Plastic Man said when we got back into the consultation room together, "what do you want to do?"

Clearly he had other patients to get to (a cool, hushed waiting room full), and he was ready to close the deal.

How was I supposed to choose a plastic surgeon when I didn't even believe in them? And how is a lay person supposed to judge surgical skill anyway? Stitch neatness and length? Maybe I should have insisted on watching him operate first. Right. I'd written whole novels about horrific bloody crimes, but I'd still faint at the first cut.

I looked at Plastic Man. He did have beautiful, scrupulously clean hands and fingers. He had the mile-long resume. He was the only one of the three plastic surgeons I'd seen who firmly said that my original idea of having the left mastectomy, a preventive one on the right, and the TRAM flap all at once was too much surgery. He definitely got points for prudence. I've learned that prudence in a surgeon is a rare thing. They generally lead with their scalpels and egos. (Although not always: the surgeon who did my adhesions operation was not only lovely, he was prudent, too.)

I couldn't keep interviewing surgeons for the rest of my life. Talk about hell. That would be it. And besides, my daughter was getting married exactly six weeks from today, and I had flowers to order, a meal to choose, fittings to attend, a fortune to spend.

"Okay, fine," I say. "Let's do it."

Plastic Man nodded blandly, told me to get dressed, and left me alone again. By the time he came back, I was dressed and crying like a baby. He seemed bewildered by this turn of events. He took me out into the minimalist hallway and deposited me in an opaque glass back office with an assistant, to whom he said, "Fran is getting a little emotional." Emotions were not, of course, his department. Cutting was his department.

I sat down at the desk and wiped my eyes with the tissue the assistant offered, then scheduled my surgery for August 20th, thirty-six hours after my daughter's wedding. The assistant handed me some papers to sign.

How did I get here and why am I signing these papers?

I signed.

PAUL WATSKY

The Healing Casebook

I

Hanuman the monkey god, grown bored with eons of unwashed mangos and consequent dysentery, composes first limerick.

II

Adult male congenitally afflicted with a single cerebral hemisphere and miniscule penis relinquishes destructive career as conservative lobbyist to travel L.A. Basin attending open mics.

III

Superlatively beautiful late-adolescent female of moderate intelligence and suffering from hypertrophic self-esteem submits work by mail to literary journals.

1V

Marginal New Hampshire farmer self-medicates for financial stress and envious anxiety by scribbling verses.

MEG NEUMAN

He has drifted back to sleep after reading the latest police procedural we purchased together. 3 minutes of tapping and sliding and it was sitting on his tablet. His resistance to getting an e-reader was well defined and he relented only when he could not muster the strength. The act of walking through the library, browsing, selecting and observing others looking for books and maybe even smelling the library interiors had been his most important life ritual. He defined every fiber and morsel of his being as atheistic but I think the library jaunts and his reading were the most spiritual and sacred part of his life.

The volume and power of his voice is nowhere near what it used to be when he stormed around at 185 lbs. and 5' 9". Almost all of his muscle mass has melted away and he now weighs 130 pounds and looks like he is 5' 5", or 5' 6", at most. His dragon veneer has disappeared piece by piece. He no longer breathes fire, only transparent oxygen through his cannula and into his nares. It is obvious that sometime during the night a tame lamb landed in his bed and climbed inside his body, extruding the remnants of the dragon who had resided there for 86 years.

He begs out of a shower every day and opts for every other day but he still takes it independently—at least this week. He has delegated watering and fertilizing the huge palm tree and peace lilies he has nourished for decades. If human and plant communication exists, then his plants are grieving his sudden disappearance and longing for his chatter-laced water to return. I am certain I have seen the palm strain to catch a glimpse of him entering the kitchen. I know their missing him will soon be mine to bear.

ALICIA OSTRIKER

Metaphor and Healing:
Or, Why Metaphor is Not a Bandage

We think we know what metaphor is, and what metaphor does. But do we? Many people think metaphor is a thing pinned to a poem like a medal on somebody's chest announcing that it is a poem. Or it is a sort of trick designed to disguise something. A fraud that masks or evades so-called "reality." Aristotle declares that "the greatest thing by far is to be a master of metaphor. It is the one thing that cannot be learned from others; and it is also a sign of genius, since a good metaphor implies an intuitive perception of the similarity in dissimilars." But I want to go further: I say metaphor is essentially erotic: it embodies the potential for healing. Metaphor is what language uses to claim that the world is full of hidden connections. Is this an extravagant or absurd claim?

To begin with, you cannot make a metaphor without caring about something enough to pay attention to it—to penetrate into its essence and discover something new there, in its depths. Or enough to look carefully at its surfaces, desiring to put the forms and colors and textures, or the smell or taste or motion of what you see, into language that is not merely technical. You cannot make a metaphor without seeing how one thing is *like* another thing. Only connect, says E. M. Forster. Make a jump, make a leap. Most of the time, we are afraid to do so, just as we are afraid to love.

METAPHOR: the etymology: a carrying across. You see the word on delivery vans in the dusty avenues of Athens. Metaphoros. A carrying across, a getting over, a bearing there. Metaphor is that which joins, that which announces connection, overlap, shared essence, and yet retains the actual distance between whatever objects it brings together.

A digression on the erotic. People who are in love famously desire to be one with the beloved. They also know that the beloved is elusive, evasive, always capable of escape. And that they themselves are also capable of escape. If they don't know it the first time around, they learn it after a while. Lovers blur into each other. Or so they believe. Yet they fail, ultimately, to fuse. They are separate beings, and they separate. Into death, says John Keats in his "Ode to Melancholy," breathing softly, ceasing upon the midnight with no pain, pillowed on his fair love's ripening breast, and so on. Poets in the Renaissance used to love to link love and death, *l'amour* and *la mort*. They called orgasm "the little death." Technically, the supposed reason was that every time a man lost some of his seed he was shortening his life. Perhaps the actual reason had something to do with a temporary loss of identity. A temporary loss, in the rapture and rupture of love, of the separation and loneliness that we carry with us from the moment we become conscious of being an "I," a self, an individual. (We of course *want* to be individuals—especially here in America—where we are all little declarations of independence, recognizing only dimly that our independence is not only a blessing but a veritable curse.)

In the myth of the garden of Eden, when Adam and Eve are expelled, God sends an angel to guard the gate with a flaming sword to prevent them from returning. Every time we fall in love, we are trying, as Joni Mitchell says, to get ourselves back to the garden. All those familiar distances and prohibitions in love stories are metaphors whose function is to amplify (as an oscillograph amplifies a tremor) and register physically (as an electron microscope registers the dotty wheeling of subatomic particles) the fundamental otherness of the beloved to the self, which however infinitely small it may become, is a distance that can never become zero. And yet, in love, one feels absolutely, momentarily or perhaps in a suffusion of feeling diffused over time, that the distance truly is zero.

So … there's my little rhapsody on the erotic. Now back to the fact that metaphor is the erotic element in language, which is why language without metaphor—medical language, for example—can be chilling and inhuman. Not that it necessarily intends this, for what it intends is precision, yet every abstract language keeps me at a distance when I want to come closer, dive in deeper, know more. It withholds information. It refuses personal intimacy. In a discourse which lacks metaphor, a disinfected discourse, which pretends to protect itself from the stains and strains of desire, the greedy exhausting disease of love, there is no mother's milk, the bread is rags, the meat is sand.

Think of legal language, mathematical language, and the language of analytic philosophy that so values logic, argumentation and evidence, is so concerned to avoid ambiguity, and stands so ready to condemn any utterance that includes emotion as "merely subjective." Think of the language of the anchorman, who is supposed to represent the news without the taint of personal feeling. Think of the codes governing medical language. How well do the codes encourage those who are caring for other human beings to care for them as human beings rather than bundles of symptoms? Metaphor on the other hand depends entirely on ambiguity, blur, the ripple effect of subjective meanings. As the generation of leaves, so the generation of men (Homer). The evening stretches out against the sky like a patient etherized upon a table (Eliot). Petals on a wet, black bough (Pound). Let me kiss you with the kisses of my mouth, for your love is sweeter than wine (The Song of Solomon). My love is like a red red rose (Robert Burns). The pleasure we take in metaphor is a pleasure of consent, an agreement that the distance between two things is cancellable because of their likeness, whereby each illuminates some inner truth belonging to the other. The question of whether the things are themselves usually pleasurable or painful is irrelevant. Metaphor is the realm not of Fact but of Truth. It is designed to make you pause, to let it sink in. Metaphor is insight. Like truth, metaphor makes pleasant all that it touches. I've used that word truth twice now, and I know we don't believe in truth any more—not absolute truth, but why not a lot of little contingent truths?

Now I want to spell out for you what I think happens in order for a metaphor to be born.

First, I desire to communicate (to you), to share (with you) my sense of some object, such as the life cycle of mankind, or an evening in which I am walking around in a city feeling miserably alienated from myself and other human beings. Second, in order to do so I must meditate further on my object, understand it more fully—in other words, I desire more of it. Its inward structure or qualities. I want to kiss it with the kisses of my mouth—that is to say, my imagination. Next, I remember that I cannot communicate what x is and means except by comparing it with non-x, but I don't yet know which non-x. The metaphor is given, comes, like an act of grace, into my consciousness. It enters with a leap and a bound. Your kisses are like ... what? Like wine, but sweeter ... My miserable mood is ... paralyzed? No, *etherized* ... and projected out into the world, into the horizontally stretched evening. Though I may have been sweating for it, frustrated as when one searches for a missing word, the search is irrelevant—it may appear without a search; and, on the contrary, any amount of search may fail to produce it. Two objects now are present; I joyously recognize their illuminating affinity, as something which really exists already in the world and was waiting to be discovered.

So here we have several sorts of desire. My desire as poet to communicate. My desire to understand x better than I do. My desire to think of a non-x which resembles x and will shed exciting light on it. Then, when I have joined my x to its non-x, the awareness that their relationship pre-existed the discovery, and *desired* to be discovered.

Can this be? Yes, it can be. Of course it always is. It always has been. *Muss es sein?* Beethoven scrawled on the manuscript of his Fifth Symphony. *Es muss sein!* But this is an old quarrel, the quarrel between those who believe the artist is one who discovers, and those who believe the artist only sticks things artificially together—or puts band-aids on reality.

Notice two things now. The two objects which a metaphor erotically joins are always at some odd asymmetrical angle to each other; they are never mere opposites, for the juxtaposition of opposites is the figure of paradox, not metaphor, nor are they from the same category of objects. There would be no point saying that a rose is like a tulip, because there is no discovery being made here. But if we say that a woman is like a rose, or that men are like leaves falling in a forest, then we are discovering that the world of plants and that of beasts are in some respects (which we do not spell out) alike, have arisen from some common source or obey common laws or manifest common features. Or if the poet Eloise Klein Healy says, "My love wants to park / in front of your house," she is discovering an affinity between the world of feeling and that of technology. When my student Chris Goodrich says, "The way a river drowns what it loves, / That's the way I love you," he is discovering something about himself, how his neediness isn't a personal thing but an impersonal one.

Now let me turn from generalizations to instances, before returning to a large generalization or so. Here is a poem entitled "Mastectomy," that deals with a single individual's experience of this procedure:

MASTECTOMY
for Alison Estabrook

I shook your hand before I went.
Your nod was brief, your manner confident,
A ship's captain, and there I lay, a chart
Of the bay, no reefs, no shoals.
While I admired your boyish freckles,
Your soft green cotton gown with the oval neck,
The drug sent me away, like the unemployed.
I swam and supped with the fish, while you
Cut carefully in, I mean
I assume you were careful.
They say it took an hour or so.

I liked your freckled face, your honesty
That first visit, when I said
What's my odds on this biopsy
And you didn't mince words,
One out of four it's cancer.
The degree on your wall shrugged slightly.
Your cold window onto Amsterdam
Had seen everything, bums and operas.
A breast surgeon minces something other than language.

That's why I picked you to cut me.

Was I succulent? Was I juicy?
Flesh is grass, yet I dreamed you displayed me
In pleated paper like a candied fruit,
I thought you sliced me like green honeydew
Or like a pomegranate full of seeds
Tart as Persephone's, those electric dots
That kept that girl in hell,
Those jelly pips that made her queen of death.

Doctor, you knifed, chopped, and divided it
Like a watermelon's ruby flesh
Flushed a little, serious
About your line of work
Scooped up the risk in the ducts
Scooped up the ducts
Dug out the blubber,
Spooned it off and away, nipple and all.
Eliminated the odds, nipped out
Those almost insignificant cells that might
Or might not have lain dormant forever.

This poem begins by using a relatively neutral, practical tone in the opening stanza, as it summarizes the speaker's experience at the time of the surgery. The metaphor of the surgeon as a ship's captain suggests confidence, technical knowledge, and the ability to direct a team; perhaps it implies the possibility of danger, as every voyage is subject to accidents. Overall, it's a metaphor that shows the speaker's respect, while the metaphor of herself as "a chart of the bay, no reefs, no shoals," is an image of passivity. She has become a thing, a geographical location, or not even that—a map of a location, an abstraction. The picture treats the upcoming surgery as something ordinary and straightforward as navigating a bay. At the same time, the "boyish freckles" of the surgeon emphasize her youth and maybe androgyny in an appealing way that gives the "ship's captain" metaphor a more tender dimension. Then, the speaker describing herself under anesthetic as being sent away "like the unemployed" emphasizes helplessness, with a sense of class structure, while "I swam and supped with the fish" moves into a dreamlike sensation of being underwater yet safe and happy, almost a womb image.

The second stanza is a flashback to the woman's first encounter with her surgeon, recounting the surgeon's directness, which the woman likes. At the same time, there are the metaphors of the surgeon's framed degree on the wall shrugging, and the window seeing "everything," creating the sense of this encounter as quite impersonal. What's a crisis for the patient is just all in the day's work for the surgeon. And what about the play on the word "mince?" On the one hand there's the idea that it's good not to "mince words," to use euphemisms of half-truths, but on the other there's the ironic association of chopping into small pieces—in this case, human flesh, which is a chilling thought.

The third stanza follows through on this, first with a much-quoted line about mortality from the Biblical prophet Isaiah (40.6), "All flesh is grass, and all the goodliness thereof is as the flower of the field," but then with the metaphors of the woman's breast "displayed" like a sweet dessert, or a sliced honeydew melon, or a seed-filled pomegranate. Here we are in the hyperbolic domain of dream, or nightmare, with grotesque suggestions of cannibalism perhaps, yet also evoking the Greek myth of Persephone, who is abducted by Hades and must remain half a year every year in the realm of death after eating pomegranate seeds he gives her. Persephone is also a goddess of fertility and renewal, for her return to earth each year brings the springtime. So this cascade of metaphors is highly complex and resonant, but the frightening image of the self as "queen of death" is dominant, with the image of the body being "knifed, chopped and divided ... like a watermelon's ruby flesh" gruesomely capping it. The succulent pleasures of candy and fruit are blended with the horror. There is no pause to recover here, for "flushed" picks up the sound of "flesh," and the poem zooms in on the instruments that "scooped ... scooped ... dug out ... spooned." Only at the very end of the poem do we discover that the cancer was in a stage so early that it might have "lain dormant forever" like an unawakened sleeping beauty. As we have become aware, ductal cancer in situ is problematic in just this way.

"Mastectomy" is a poem I wrote six months after my own mastectomy, in 1991. It is the fourth in a series of poems telling the story of my surgery and recovery, published in my book *The Crack in Everything* in 1996. It took six months of healing before I was ready to begin these poems, but once they began I was determined to revise and polish them scrupulously because I knew if I could make good poems out of them they would be useful to others. To a great extent, this meant finding the right metaphors, finding language that would somehow capture the complicated and very mixed emotions accompanying the trauma of losing a breast. Other factors were important, of course—the mock-jaunty tone, the narrative structure, the cadences, rhymes and off-rhymes. But without its metaphors, this poem would be meaningless. With the metaphors, the event of a mastectomy was rendered with the bizarre intensity it seemed to require, and it was also anchored in contexts beyond itself—a ship, a map of a bay, the world underwater which so much resembles a womb, the world of medical school, the world of Amsterdam Avenue in New York, Biblical language, succulent fruit, a myth of death and fertility, a hint of gambling. All these metaphoric contexts were brought implicitly into connection. No reader of the poem would have to be conscious of the connections, but they would be present, just below the level of consciousness. And that is how metaphor works.

The implication of every metaphor is that the world is a multidimensional web of connections between animate and inanimate, larger and smaller, past and present, human and animal and vegetable and mineral, which await discovery. Every metaphor hints at universal metaphor. Is there any kind of objective basis for all this? Every religion says yes—at least at a mystical level. In the "objective" physical world it is true that all objects attract each other gravitationally, and in some cases magnetically as well, and at a subatomic level bits of matter compel one another through strong and weak forces behaving selectively. But also, in every metaphor the two compared objects retain their own qualities and histories. So there is always simultaneously likeness and difference, fusion and separation.

The poet Jane Hirshfield has said, "There is only one real reason to read a poem, and that is to find your way to a larger life than would otherwise be yours to live. This is also the only reason to write a poem." Metaphor enlarges us by letting us reach across chasms. As each of us is locked within the self, to reach across becomes part of the work of healing.

JOAN BARANOW

By Now

from your grave
wisps of grass
as sparse as your pale hair.

Down there,
your body is busy
feeding roots.

Isn't that what mothers do?

You cook inside a strange kitchen
in a dark house.

These six years—
as if you'd just stepped away
to turn the oven off.

In Case You'd Like to Know

We were all there,
bereaved and bewildered,
fumbling the forms of ritual—
a poem, an aria, a picture
and flowers balanced on the box
that held you hovering
over the draped hole.
The winter sun was there,
the ground brittle with pine.
We kept sighing, resigned.

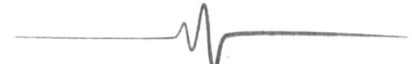

Checking Margins

She went in twice to be sure
and found nothing more
like going back to check a cold stove.
Gas is invisible to the casual eye,
the same as breast cancer,
until the cells start elbowing each other,
spilling drinks, scattering crumbs
across the mammography floor.
By then the only recourse is eviction,
for which preparation must be made,
poisons procured. Ever after
the world is weirdly foreshortened,
like that picture of the star
far in the past that blew
10 billion years ago, whose light
is just now reaching this room.

February & plum trees in bloom

girlish trees, they are always
ready first,
they toss their skimpy skirts to the ground

all the way down Blithedale Ave,
between carports and fences,
the annual Rapture

and let's not forget freesias & narcissus
in the supermarkets,
bundled & thrust into tubs
stacked by the automatic entrance

a sort of heaven's floral gate?

I watch us pass in and out, preoccupied,
I, too, hurried along,
my heart an empty wrapper

blown among petals opening lavender wings

SUZANNE TAY-KELLEY

Gelato

why so I fear wiping a tear from a stranger's glistening cheek?
why do I fear chastising a nun who could never hope to be pope?
why do I fear dancing my poetry naked in the Trevi?

what if I knew this mocha gelato would be my final scoop?
fear would be vapor and
I'd lick my spoon

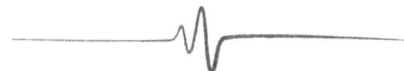

Starstruck

the stars are out and you are near
your wits are clear, my cares have flown
invite the moon and grab a beer
the stars are out and you are near
I can scarcely contain my neon cheer
please don't mind the occasional moan
the stars are out and you are near
your wits are clear, my cares have flown

First Date

an emerald Pinto our Pegasus steed
wings us to beach where we splay grand buffet
brie-grades-merlot in Pacific-bit breeze
weave poppies and lupines in fragrant bouquet

spry smile swallows fog, snatches swank sun
cream voice enthralls, bewitches with tales
before us, sea swings, sails overrun
surging slate sheet of glistening swells

below, an ephemeral blue sheens sand
we race into surf of cold stabbing knives
touch wails taste echoes of jellies, thousands
stranded by tide, wrecked indigo lives

tear-splashed fingers in his hands he folds
sapphire sky ignites crimson go

SUSAN MOLDAW

Spinning Through the Heavens

When I entered the patient's room the first thing I saw was his naked, round stomach swelling over his pajama bottoms and embellished with a scatter of tattoos that looked like ancient symbols. I fought my discomfort and asked if I could sit down, because that's what chaplains do. He said all right, so I pulled up a chair and faced him. He was sitting on the side of his bed, looking out a window that showcased the city buildings adjacent to the hospital. The TV was on. He was in his late twenties and had been admitted with an infection, but the underlying disease was cystic fibrosis, a serious condition whose sufferers usually die early.

"I just bought a guitar," he told me and described the make, model, and style, saying it was a "good deal." His body wriggled in a quick, unconscious dance to music from the TV. When I told him, he laughed.

"I like music," he said and then: "I always knew I'd die young. Sometimes I wish it would just hurry up."

I asked him if he had a plan for suicide, as I'd been trained. He laughed and said, "No, it's not like that."

"When did you learn you had a terminal condition?" I said.

"As long as I can remember. I figured by the time I was twenty-four or twenty-five, I'd be dead."

I wondered what it would be like to know you're going to die before your time, and as if in answer to my unstated question, he went on.

"I partied and did drugs with my friends, and then I looked around at twenty-four and realized I'm still here. I decided to clean myself up. I moved but that didn't help. You take yourself with you. I've been trying to change. I'm just glad now to wake up, sit in the sun, drink coffee."

"You're taking responsibility for yourself."

"Oh—I don't know. I just said it because it sounded good."

I burst into laughter and he smiled, looking at me for the first time. He had a boyish face and tousled, light brown hair. When I looked past the scars and tattoos and his disheveled appearance, he reminded me of one of my sons. I knew enough to remind myself he wasn't—that mother instinct is hard to shake.

Two nurses came into his room to replace a catheter in his chest. I asked if he wanted me to leave but he said no, scooting to the top of the bed and sitting against the wall, with his legs under the covers, so the nurses could do their job. He asked why there were two, and the head nurse explained she was training a student.

"I'd rather have the pro," he said, and the head nurse assured him she'd be in charge. He and the nurse had a technical discussion about veins and catheter placement in medical lingo that I didn't understand. He rested his head on the pillow as she put in the line. His eyes were closed and his breathing was slow and measured. There was no betrayal of pain, until I looked at his feet and saw his toes, curling and uncurling under the sheet. I looked at his face and saw a slight grimace, and then it was over.

When the nurses finished, he sat up and nodded. "Thank you," he said, with the grace of a king.

"You've been doing this a long time," I said, after they left.

"All my life."

And then the conversation turned. He told me that just before he went to the hospital, he was picked up by the police when he was walking down an alley. They searched him and didn't find much, he said, just some pot and "a line of crystal meth." He went before a judge, who sentenced him to weekly classes on drug abuse.

"I explained to him that I had medical needs and couldn't always make the classes, but they don't care."

And then, in spite of myself, I wanted to know if his mother took care of him when he was young, so I asked. He wasn't sure what I meant.

"My biological parents split up," he said. "I never see my dad. My mom— yeah—she was busy partying. My uncle was the one who took me to games and threw a baseball and made sure I took my meds. He's the kind of guy who would beat the shit out of my mom's boyfriends." His eyes narrowed and his voice got husky. "He went to prison. When he got out, something changed." From the hallway I heard someone ask for water. A cleaning person pushed a cart. Without looking at me, he continued. "He committed suicide. Maybe he was depressed. I know he felt bad he couldn't support his family. That's all I can think of."

He got up and sat on the side of the bed again, staring out the window and wiping his eyes with his hands.

"You felt close to him," I said.

He kept looking at the view. "Yeah. I don't usually talk about this stuff. Don't want to be a downer."

"It's hard to keep it all inside."

"That's what I do."

"Thanks for talking with me," I said.

"Thanks for listening." He looked at me, almost surprised.

The next day I stopped by, but he waved me away. He was too tired, he said. I overheard one of the nurses telling another nurse he should be in hospice. A day later I knocked and went in. He was sitting in a chair. There was a guitar in a stand in the corner of his room.

"I don't have anything to say," he said.

I asked about the guitar and he told me a friend brought it by—his only normal friend, someone who didn't do drugs, a nurse.

"The doctor said we need to be talking about the end of life," he said.

I told him I felt sad, hearing that.

"Yeah. I don't talk with my father, and my mother, she tries, but she doesn't have the money to get down to see me."

I felt a rush of maternal anger. If he were my son I'd be there, no question. I had a sudden urge to tuck him into bed and smooth his covers, the way I would with one of my sons if he were sick.

"You want your mother with you," I said. He said yeah, and his eyes got narrow and squinty.

"I get the sense you feel pretty alone right now."

"Yeah." And then: "I like it that way."

He said he was tired so I left. The next day he waved to me in the hallway. I went in his room. He was folding clothes, wearing a black T-shirt and gym shorts. The window was open, and the room felt fresh and breezy. He was laughing. I sat down in the chair by the bed.

"I just got off the phone with my father," he said. "He's got plans. He's going to get a hold of the doctor and find out what's going on. I hope to hell he doesn't piss the doctor off." He put some clothes in a drawer and looked at me. "I just wish for one day my family would come into the hospital and see what I go through—the tests, the doctors, the X-rays. But—it's selfish, maybe. I don't think they would."

"Why not?"

"They wouldn't take the day. I wouldn't do it." He shook his head and his eyes got teary. "Only my uncle." He sat across from me on the bed. "I hate to say it," he said. "We're white trash." He grinned and patted his stomach. "I'm in no hurry to get out of here. The food's pretty good. I need to take care of myself. I asked my nurse-friend how much time I had left. Five years? She said I had at least a year. I figure I have a year to be myself before things go downhill."

"What does it mean to be yourself?" I said, thinking: five years has the ring of eternity. When my father was dying, he longed for five, but he, too, got the one-year reply.

"I'm a twenty-nine-year-old young man with cystic fibrosis who desperately needs a girlfriend." His eyes sparkled, and at that moment he looked like any guy his age whose biggest concern was getting a girl into bed.

I went to see him again, but the nurse said he had been discharged. Leaving the hospital that night I remembered what he told me about his tattoos. His uncle did the work; he learned how to tattoo in prison. I asked if it hurt to get them, and he said no. Then I asked him to tell me what they meant.

"This one here," he said, pointing to the top one, "it's the peace sign, upside down. The middle one is a bolt of lightning."

I saw that now. "And the bottom tattoo?" I said.

"It's a planet and those are flames underneath."

I looked more closely at the swirling blue ink. "It's like a star on fire," I said, "spinning through the heavens."

His eyes shone with the pleasure of being understood, then his expression hardened.

"Yeah," he said. "It's like that."

ERIC CHANG

Rosina on the table

The anesthetist raises a finger
to her like I curse the fork
that backs the drain. I am
stained in blood and bile
and nothing romantic. My hand
is on her leg and she
is refusing to wake.

We believe she cannot
be dreaming in her state
but we are all clinging
to something in that room.
I dream of hostels and Soweto
running you home the night
hard and homebrew
on my breath. You with
something threatening yet
manageable maybe diabetes
maybe celiac. Breaking
into our parents' bedrooms
and masquerading in God's Own
Cosmetics.

I no longer find your
appearance beautiful now

I imagine conversations
and your understanding of
what it means to be
so incredibly full. Blue
eyes and what I thought
milk only night air.

Soneto LXVI

My American-born friends
said two different things:
that those south of the equator
know the cold as "summer"
or that their "winter" falls
at the opposite time. Like
el rayo de Enero could burn
you up or stand you up
and in every case you
miss her.

I'd imagined the equator as
a glass-bottomed boat: everyone
improbably inverted underneath.
Our feet swiping in balletic
kicks or socks-off embraced.
The way we drove the magnet
below to lead the iron car
down miniature streets, our dance
electric and theirs more foos—
like molecular structures, at once
erratic, graceful, stiff.

I guess my thesis this time
is this: the opposites twin
in every way except
one. Black in its absence,
white in its excess, all held
for the overwhelming
presence of color.

There exist unusual knots
for tying people together. My South
American sister hurdles
at the same trajectory but toward

an un-ringed target. Her immigrant
grandfather never held a firearm;
her mother's indigenous
love infinite but perfectly
enough.

My *sudoamericano* counterpart
still apologizes only when
appropriate. He hopes to be
better yet accepts who he
is. And he has you and holds you
until your mouth is
open, whispers love inside. Then
means it.

Range

Those were not gunshots, that first
night in the city, during my hardwood
meal. Nor in Obs, as Thabo told
me of the Wynberg girl with birdshot
in her eye.

Davis says never to pull or strain. Only
squeeze, such that each shot is
a surprise. Only a lesson in masking,
such that when the accused
swear no authority over their bullets,
some truth.

What Davis doesn't know is that I have
always split timelines. I tear them from
the air with my hands. Much like
now, the work is heavy and hot, like
caring for a dying sun.

This universe glows, recoils. In the other
we also expand, but it's manageable—we
are the descendants of Abel. In the other
we don't dream another universe inside us,
and when asked, I know exactly where
my joy is.

DEBORAH STEINBERG

Pain Map

The technician mapped my pain with needles and hands, points corresponding to other points like Napa and Bordeaux, or San Francisco and Cape Town. Resonating frequencies: pain suddenly audible, seeking harmonies. These relationships were then projected visually onto an expanse of white wall: *Look this is the planet of your body,* she said, *The planet of your body stretched flat to two dimensions, thus necessarily distorted, though color has been used to show some relief.*

I saw continents, I saw oceans, I saw exploding volcanoes and valleys bursting with plenty. I saw no borderlines no regulations no visas no landmines. I saw cities emitting toxic fumes and bridges connecting landmasses. I saw fishermen plying the open waters in boats precariously fragile for the sea. I saw dragons threatening where the edges dropped into void and four puffy-cheeked winds in the corners stirring it all up. My pain-map looked like it had been executed by a fourteenth-century monk using tempera paint, dimensionality expressed with different colors rather than shading, small monsters and gargoyles adding a nice personal touch to the work. The whole thing hummed and creaked and strained toward harmony: sailors sang sea shanties, migrant workers sang labor ballads, and mothers cradled lullabies in the safe snugness of their palates.

As you can see, the technician said, *the map requires little explanation.*

Pain was a continent almost blindingly bright, a scorched land that bled into the water channels and polluted the other continents until none was free of its blight. *Now watch*, the technician said, and began turning fluorescent dials on the bio-cartography machine. The pain continent slowly morphed into a brightly-plumed tropical bird, heaved itself from the map's glossy surface, screeched magnificently, and winged heavily out the open window, gaining altitude with every beat, until it became indistinguishable from the sun.

Pain still inhabited my body, for a map is not the terrain it describes, but it had loosened, become willing, perhaps, to depart like that variegated bird in whose vanished shadow I still lay, watching the map full of colors and motion: a planet, an ecosystem, in the process of healing itself.

The High Wind

A company has begun bottling the high wind to sell on the luxury market. I was given a bottle (blue-tinged glass, contemporary design) by a well-meaning relative, but can't bring myself to drink it. High wind compressed in glass and sipped on the ground couldn't possibly set the whole body humming with the clean perfume of risk the way it does when one hovers just at the top of human flight range. It would be diluted or, worse, a laboratory-synthesized imitation for those who believe the sublime can be manufactured. Worse, still: even authentic, unadulterated high wind might pale to bland against the romance of its dream flavor, which lingers on my tongue when I wake, spiced with pine, sugared with snow from distant summits, distilled as whisky, complex as wine.

But more: once drunk, I would lack even the imagined stirring of the wind in its carefully designed prison. So I keep the bottle next to my head while I sleep, to remind me of that high country where no foot can tread, that country which is more beautiful since I cannot return.

Balcony

These wings are rusty from disuse, smelling of mothballs and dusty acrylic fur, wilting from lack of light. These muscles are stiff from forced stasis, joints refusing to roll, aching to turn in their sockets and stretch their fibers for flight, yes, flight will eventually follow. First steps stumbling to sever ties with the earth; first fumbling flapping then falling back down; first tragic takeoff terminated, but back up for another attempt.

The physical therapist says the pain is part of it; it has to hurt before it heals. Don't focus on the time lost, she says, fix the horizon with your eyes: that's where you're bound. One morning you'll spring from the ground without a thought, and this dusty trail you're forced to walk at present will wilt below you, become a single hair fallen from your head and already forgotten. Sing to your muscles of that morning as you coax them open, sing songs of freedom to soften this petrified body. Sung while at work, songs sometimes become prayers, praising the potential hidden in the body to heal itself—and more, to forgive the apathy that led to atrophy.

They are dull and matted, yellowed like old letters. It would be easiest to hide their shame under an overcoat, let them go another day, another year, until they wither and fall like blossoms gone unnoticed all spring then longed for in the dry months. But this morning I'll get out the shampoo and the perfume, draw a bath and scrub vigorously, let the hot water work on the rigid tendons. Then draw the curtains back and, in my best new clothes, stand on the balcony. It is not leaping I have planned for the moment, but looking:

Towards that old horizon.

MARILYN KRYSL

Litany

Poems, Donald Hall writes, are pleasure first: bodily pleasure, a deliciousness of the senses. Language "works" on an intellectual level, but it is the miracle of our sense of hearing that offers us the bodily, rhythmic, sounding pleasure Hall invokes. Think of poetry then as spoken music, spoken song. Even if you are writing free verse, you want the poem to sing and drum its imagery and its wisdom.

Two attributes that create poetry's "sonic singing" are repetition and variation.

Poets, like musicians, live between these two poles. The recurring of sunrise and sunset, noon and midnight, solstice and equinox—these repeating events soothe us, just as do repeating sounds and rhythms in music and poetry.

Generally speaking, repetition and variation both need equal time in a given poem. Too much repetition for too long can become a soporific and put us to sleep. Then we long for variation, which delivers potent, new, bold, adventurous energy.

To say it another way: Repetition makes us feel safe and variation makes us feel free and expansive.

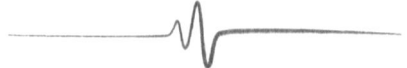

Litany began as a form of prayer in which the clergy and the congregation acted out call and response. Each line of a litany begins with a repeating phrase and ends with a variant image, as in Margaret Wise Brown's children's book *Goodnight Moon*:

> Goodnight comb
> Goodnight brush
> Goodnight nobody
> Goodnight mush

In Anne Waldman's thirty-page "Fast Speaking Woman" she describes herself:

> I'm an abalone woman
> I'm the abandoned woman
> I'm the woman abashed, the gibberish woman,
> The aborigine woman, the woman absconding ...

When I was commissioned by Jean Watson at The Center for Human Caring to write poems that described caregivers and their work, I wrote a litany to invoke our bodies, bodies which need another's human touch in order to heal.

SKIN

Because skin is the first organ
    to form in the womb, and first things
    are of first importance

Because skin is the largest
    organ—an adult's skin weighs six pounds
    and stretched out covers eighteen square feet—

Because the skin's resilience
    can only be experienced

Because it feels superior by far
    to silk or challis

and in addition is lovely
to look at, nothing by Cardin
comes close to it

Because it's the organ with which we experience wind,
which most loves water,

Because it's the organ through which we begin
to discover each other

because, because, because, and for all these good reasons

hurry out and touch someone now! Delay
in this matter is not
a good idea, you have delayed too long
already, your suffering brothers and sisters
are waiting, you can hardly expect them to wait
much longer, and remember, when you touch
another person, the skin
gives off a chemical which makes them, and you
feel better
more alert
more cheerful
more willing to take chances
more open to new experience
more generally obstreperously intent on securing
the greatest good for everybody
and more likely to say NO to the B-1 Lancer bomber
and YES to the levy for the public schools.

After all, it's
the organ

through which we take in
the light we give out

The "*because*" litany begins the poem so that the hearer may anchor in
the comfort of its repetition. Then the poem shifts us to the eight line

passage of variation so that we may feel free and expansive. And then near the finale, there appears again the five line litany of "more." What has happened is that we have experienced a satisfying balance between repetition and variation. The poem leaves us in the best of both worlds. In my poem "Saying Things" I used the litany form to praise the beauty, robustness and superfluity of single words.

> Three things quickly, pineapple, sparrow grass, whale
> and then on to asbestos. What I want to say tonight
> is words, the naming of things into their thing,
> yucca, brown sugar, solo, the roll of a snare drum,
> say something, anything, you'll see what I mean ...

The poem continues its love song to language for thirty-five more lines, and the litany of the word "say" keeps sounding. Its power is balanced by the words that follow and complete each line.

In a third example of litany there are two players: the right and left hands, images for two potentials, the potential for cooperation and harmony and the potential for antagonism and destruction.

POEM FOR THE LEFT AND RIGHT HANDS

> The left hand trails in the water
> The right is tying knots
>
> The right stitches a seam
> The left sleeps in the silk
>
> The right eats
> The left listens under the table
>
> The right swears
> The left wears the rings
>
> The right wins, the right loses
> The left holds the cards
> The left strikes chords while the right
> runs, runs, up and down, up and down

and when the right can't sleep and travels
around the world against the clock
the left is buried

Oh left hand, you're so quiet
Do you have children, a dog, mistresses, debts

It's the right that buys the groceries
shifts gears
runs for high office
feeds the baby little silver spoonfuls
It's the right that grabs the knife
to hack off the left hand

The left hand waits
a blind dog

holding in its mouth
the right's glove

The knife falls, clatters
The left hand is the right's

Only chance

Repetition and variation make their appearance, dance briefly, then step back, so that the emotional thrust of the poem's action can play out to its conclusion.

Think of the repetition in rap lyrics. Think of Spoken Word. Litany is both primordial and modern. We see it in women who take up knitting to stitch themselves into the community of space/time. Litany has been with us since the first birds appeared on the planet. It has been with us since the first humans gripped a stone in each hand and clapped the two stones together. It has been with us since the first being stretched animal hide over a frame to make a drum. The shaman's drum called all beings together, called them to consciousness of each other and of the whole community. We still hear that same primordial drum.

JOANNE CLARKSON

The Oldest Sense
For Freida

I meet you as I tape your face
back together. Your eyes and
remnant lips beg for this single
thing: a memory like roses
> *for my faithful*
> *husband; for my impressionable*
> *children*

Cancer eats like acid, harsh and
sloppy. Bandages deceive the eyes
but not the clever nose. Smell

is the oldest sense. It fetals in the limbic
brain like the collective sigh
of ancestors. It tells us when
we're sick.
The best doctor I ever knew
> diagnosed with breath

and now you, my challenging
patient.
> *Don't let them dread*
> *me*, you beg in halting syllables
> of untethered bone.

I promise what my powders and salve,
candles and spray can only partially
erase. Are there miracles for cells
that eat themselves?

We know blindfolded the sweat
of a mate, skin of children
the coming of rain
incense of death.

I tape the last of the gauze
in place and call to what is older still
than sound, taste, fingers, vision
or scent.

They Had Already Made Love

Well into February, the waning winter, down
the lane to the home closest to the river, I drive
with my Home Health wisdoms:

>What to do after your chest
>is cracked open, the heart's blood
>re-valved and re-mapped, a new
>electric pendulum embedded.
>Miracle or massacre?

They sit together, husband and his almost
widow, their many years in pictures and chipped
paint scattered around them. Their hands cling
knuckle-white to this side of nothingness.

I open my nursing bag of –scopes and –ometers,
devices for listening to pronounce him sound
two days beyond the hospital. Then begin
the god lists as though heart is soul:

>Thou shalt not lift. No fats. No hot baths.
>No sex for at least six weeks

I glance up meeting their startled blush
and know they have already done it: consummated
resurrection, the nurture of lust. I
pretend not to notice, tell them to live
well, to do what feels right

>drive away rejoicing that the heart,
>truly mended,
>never waits.

Watching for Morning

There's a tide to all this: seventeen
houseboats rock the harbor,
waking to gulls. I watch from
the bank above, nesting the way
I often do, in my mind's eye.

I see the shudder of a small red
door that sticks a little then swings.
A figure—she—I can tell
it's a woman under baggy plaid,
sweeps the deck, tidies, readying the day.

Then she stands, just stands, legs
slightly apart for balance, looking west not
east, arms slack. She

has lost someone. A man
most likely and with him her
womanhood. Children by a first love
who have given themselves away.

Out on open water, the first canvas lifts,
unfurls and is pregnant with wind.
Journey is brisk, bucking. I can
tell she longs for sail even more than
for a mate. I would send her one
if I could, then take her place
on the houseboat at dawn.

LEEANN BARTOLINI

French Kissing the Earth

It has taken me
half a life
to fall in love again
and now I want to sleep on you,
go deep inside
be tangled in your gnarled roots—
let the sage colored moss weave
braids into my curly hair
and the dirt of your surface fill
my nails with desire.
I want to know more
about your wildness.
Name the stone, bird, star.
Share conversations over
moonlight and let
your berry raindrops
fill my starving, naked soul.

HER EYES

Father	could
not	donate
HER	EYES
to	science,
see	them
leave	her
body	along
with	heart,
lung,	liver.
HER	EYES
linger	with
the	emptied
vessel	of
her	body.
In	my
dream	forty
years	later
HER	EYES
startle	me—
even	though
we	leave,
parts	remain.

Starting to work the California garden in winter

Crackle of thin ice is heard from under my work boots
A six-sided star shoots outward, with a soft center of saffron
and the Narcissus are here
What remain of last autumn's apples dangle from the tree
Grey galvanized pails hold days of frozen rainwater
Deer dawdle around the garden gate
Spider sparkles in her web
as morning sun hits her head
Trowel strikes the hardened soil
like lumber that will not shatter
the dirt below does not alter

Press toe on hem of shovel
dig deeper in this corner
uncover a moving muck
of bug infested earth
be made present
to all that lives
underneath.

KATIE AMATRUDA

Something Always Knows

The snakes slither. Black crosses cover their bodies. In the presence of evil, the snakes contract. When they sense good, they weave and dance across the sand, leaving trails of gold, and fractals of light.

I have to gather the light.

This desert is the place of no life. The snakes must find their way out. If they stay here, the body will die.

All is silent except for the sound of a machine, and, under that, maybe a faint heartbeat.

My hands are tied down because I keep trying to pull out the tubes. Fever blazes despite the cooling blanket. A ventilator pushes air into my lungs, breathing for me, as blood and gunk pour out. A tube to bring nutrition is threaded through my nose; it had earlier caused a massive nosebleed, which, combined with a low red blood cell count, necessitated transfusions. A catheter takes away urine, which is bloody. Compression stockings pump on my swollen legs, to prevent blood clots. An arterial line is sutured into my wrist, so they can get blood from an artery to check the oxygen levels. Tubes pierce my arms, bringing in drugs: to kill bacteria, to stop wheezing, to cut the pain, to stop blood from clotting, and to make me forget. Especially to forget—Versed, Valium, Vecuronium, Haldol, and later morphine course through IVs so that I lose consciousness, am paralyzed, and to keep the horror of what is happening to the body from getting to the mind.

But something knows. Something always knows.

It's hard to say my body; the impulse is still, after so many years, to say, "the body," to dissociate. I wasn't there, I was having visions.

I was in a desert. I was with snakes, their trails glittering with light, or shepherded by angels with wings of silk, their caresses on my cheeks so tender that even today the memory brings tears to my eyes. No, I wasn't that body, tied down, dead but for the machines. That wasn't me.

I had just had a baby, a beautiful, healthy, 9 lb. 10 oz. baby boy named Colety Joseph. Labor had been a bitch—it was everything you pray won't happen when you give birth to your child. I had back labor, stalled labor, morphine so I could rest and recoup my strength, and my water had to be broken. Two epidurals and Pitocin were administered. After forty-four hours of ineffective labor, four hours of pushing, and still no baby, vacuum forceps were used, and failed. When fetal monitors indicated distress to the baby, I had a Caesarian section.

I remember thinking, as I was freezing cold, shaking, under the too bright lights on the operating table, a very simple, very protective, and probably very destructive thought, "This isn't happening to me."

I was far, far away. I saw a baby arching his back over the curtain and the blue curly slickness of the umbilical cord. The doctors were joking, saying he'd be a football player, "Even if his head had come out, his shoulders would've gotten stuck." They called it cephalopelvic disproportion, meaning his head was too big for my pelvis.

The surgeons handed the baby to other doctors, who passed him to my husband, Roy, who brought him over to me. Colety had clear, clear eyes. I had been trying for twelve years to get pregnant; he was our miracle. It was April 22nd. He was born at 2:37 a.m.

I held him in the recovery room, nursed him, shielding him from the harsh lights by making a tent for us with a hydrangea-colored paper gown. The light filtered blue as I gazed in wonder at those pure eyes. He had a conehead from the failed vacuum forceps, and his nose was pugged from the back labor. His hair was black and coarse and he had a little, red wrinkled face. The poor guy was a mess and my heart cracked open wide enough to hold the whole world just looking at him.

I had a fever. At first, it was unnoticed by staff, then they sent me down for an x-ray and I couldn't get off the x-ray table by myself. The technician didn't help; he'd already left the room. I lay there, in pain from my C-section incision, finally crawling down, and somehow I hauled myself into the wheelchair. I sat in the ugly hallway, sobbing, until Roy found me.

The baby had a fever too. They came to take him away and I couldn't stop them. I was too weak to cry out, and Roy was asleep, so I threw a book at him to wake him up. He was mad at me for doing that. They took the baby anyway and returned him with his little arm splinted and strapped down to an IV. I cried, seeing my son, only a few hours old, knowing that he had felt pain. He also had the shakes, so they kept pricking him to check his blood sugar. We both had FUOs—Fevers of Unknown Origin.

I wept more, and they diagnosed me with hormones. No one understood I was crying because they had put my baby in the intensive care nursery. My fever continued to climb, and blood cultures were ordered. They sent a portable x-ray to the room when it was clear I could not walk anywhere. They put me on oxygen and Albuterol to help with breathing.

I remember only the heat of the fever, the pain of the wound and wanting my son. I would doze, deliriously come to, say, "Where is my baby?" and sink back into my febrile dreams.

Colety and I are on a journey together, on a ship. It's an old wooden ship, with many sails, like a pirate ship. I don't know where we are going. Deep blue waters surround us as we glide over the sea.

Day 2: April 23

My fever continued to rise, and I was too weak to walk. Again, they wheeled the x-ray machine to my bed. The x-rays showed a deteriorating situation. What had begun as a left lower lobe density—probably pneumonia—

had spread to the right lung, and there was evidence of congestive heart failure, and possibly the partial collapse of a lung.

Day 3: April 24

Another chest x-ray showed continued worsening in my lungs. Roy left mid-afternoon to coach a Little League game and to have dinner with his kids, Kira and Evan. He must not have known how sick I was becoming, or he wouldn't have gone. They transferred me to the Critical Care Unit after diagnosing a "significant pulmonary problem."

Machines roared, whirred, and hummed. It felt too noisy for Colety and me; me somehow, in my delirium, believing they would bring a baby into the critical care unit. They stuck a hard plastic tube of oxygen up my nose and yelled at me when I took it out, because it hurt. I kept asking for my son, kept repeating, "Where's my baby?" They wouldn't bring him to me, wouldn't tell me how he was.

Another X-ray was taken, and this one showed "bilateral air-space consolidation ... most consistent with pulmonary edema." This meant my lungs were getting worse: where oxygen was supposed to be, there was fluid or solid material. Pulmonary edema leads to shortness of breath, and is usually caused by heart failure.

Of course, I didn't know any of the x-ray results. All I knew was that I had been transferred to this loud place, away from my son, and my husband was gone. Speaking was hard, due to the shortness of breath. I could only get out two to three words at a time, gasping, "My baby?" I was afraid he was very sick, and that they were lying to me.

A nurse came in and I begged for ice for my Caesarian section wound, which hurt. A lot. My abdomen had been cut open, my uterus pulled out of my body, sliced apart and shoved back in, after removing a giant baby, and I was being given no pain medication. That was cruel. I asked for ice for the intense pain, but secretly I was planning to suck on the ice, because they were "keeping me dry" for possible intubation, although I didn't know that at the time. I just knew they wouldn't give me any water or ice and I was burning up with fever and had never been so thirsty in my life. They didn't bring me the ice.

I called my older brother, Tom, in L.A. He and his wife had just arrived in Desert Hot Springs with their infant son Jake, escaping the smoke of the Rodney King Riots. He told me later that I said, "The doctor is trying to control me. I'm going to pull out my IV and my oxygen and go and get the baby and wait for Roy in the parking lot." It was primal; I knew only that I needed to get out of there, with Colety, or something bad would happen.

My brother, who is a doctor, called my doctor, who said I needed to be intubated. Then Tom called my father, who is also a doctor, and my dad somehow tracked down Roy. He scared Roy enough that Roy raced back from the Little League game, saying later he'd never driven so fast in his life. My brother called my sister Chris in Berkeley, across the Bay, and said, "Go, now! She is refusing to be intubated, and she may die." Chris popped her four-month-old daughter in the car seat and took off, speeding. She and Molly made that drive, over one hundred miles, round trip, many times during my hospitalization.

The doctor came in to see me, spitting mad. She yelled at me for calling my brother. She said, "You have hypoxia … not enough oxygen to the brain. We may have to intubate you."

I said, "Over my dead body."

She said, "It may come to that. If we don't, you might die."

I found out later, from my brother, that he suspected that the doctor's plan was that if I continued to refuse to be intubated, and Roy could not be located, that she would wait until I either passed out from lack of oxygen or had a cardiac arrest, and then she would intubate me. If you are unconscious, then you have given implied consent to a life-saving medical procedure. She would be able to do this because I hadn't signed a DNR—Do Not Resuscitate—order, nor did I have an Advanced Directive on file.

X-rays showed a complete whiteout of my lungs. I had ARDS—Adult Respiratory Distress Syndrome, a life-threatening lung condition that prevents enough oxygen from getting to the lungs and into the blood. People die from ARDS.

They didn't know the origin of my ARDS, so they weren't sure how to treat it. Was the source an embolus of amniotic fluid that had injured the lungs? After a Caesarian section, fluid from the birth can get into the veins and enter the lungs, causing extreme damage by a chemical reaction—a rare but catastrophic event with a high mortality rate. Was it caused by pneumonia? Or endometritis, which is an infection in the lining of the uterus, perhaps from childbirth? All of this was complicated by hypoxemia—an abnormally low concentration of oxygen in the blood, the fever, extreme swelling in my limbs, the Caesarian section, a racing heartbeat, and possible congestive heart failure.

I still refused to be intubated; I had so little oxygen going to my brain, all my thoughts were fixated on getting to my son. It made perfect sense to me at the time; if I was intubated, I couldn't be with him, in the intensive care nursery, so of course I said no to the procedure.

The doctor's notes say:

> Patient's pulmonary status has clearly deteriorated with respiratory rate 40-50 [Normal range is 12-18 breaths per minute.] Patient is acutely ill, agitated, anxious. Does not believe MDs (me) are being honest with her. I have had extensive discussions with the patient, her father, her brother, her sister. Intubation is necessary secondary to ARDS. I have asked anesthesia to intubate—I believe patient will allow another MD to do this more easily than she would allow me.

It was night when Roy came tearing in. They explained to him that I had Adult Respiratory Distress Syndrome. The doctor told Roy that treatment for ARDS needed to be started to reduce the risk of death and to prevent further damage to my lungs and other organs. The goal was to keep me alive and breathing while finding out and treating whatever had caused the ARDS.

The doctor told him that I needed to be placed on a ventilator to stay alive. With ARDS, the oxygen in the blood drops quickly to dangerously low levels, causing damage to vital organs and even severe brain damage. Intubation could save my life.

I saw Roy, and that was the last thing I remembered, consciously, for the next ten days. He gave them permission to intubate me, and at 9:00 p.m. on April 24th, I was sedated and an endotracheal tube was pushed down my throat into my trachea. I was sedated and paralyzed and put into a type of medically induced coma. I was gone.

There is a moment between the end of the day and the beginning of the night, a space between, a place between. There is a world where worlds meet, a moment between the awakening and the dream, a place between night and morning. There is a world where worlds meet, a moment between the dream and the awakening, between dawn and dusk, in the place between sleep and waking. The veils between worlds are thin here. It is the threshold. Cross it.

Later that night, they told Roy that I had a less than fifty percent chance of surviving. He went and held our baby, and then spent time with me. He ended up at the chapel, trying to sleep, and talking to God. He prayed that I wouldn't die and that our son would have a mother.

Colety was in the neonatal intensive care unit, struggling with his fever.

Day 4: April 25

My body was intubated, with a catheter for urine output, and an IV bringing in medications including three different antibiotics, and Versed and Vecuronium, two paralytics. Fevers continued. Coarse crackles sounded in both lungs. My abdomen was distended and soft. White blood cell counts increased, meaning infection was present. A sample was taken from my lungs to rule out viral, fungal, and Legionella bacteria as the cause for the ARDS.

I feel the wings of the angels of childbirth caress my cheeks like the softest silk. I cry; it is so tender. They reassure me that they will be there for Colety if I die.

But where is my baby?

Is he dead?

My brother Tom arrived, much to Roy's relief. My brother consulted with the doctor, who told him, "She's going to hate me. Patients always hate the doctor who intubates them."

Tom told me later that he was quite heartened by two things:

1. My lungs were not stiff. He thought, "That's totally great. I was used to people whose lungs got stiff when they were intubated, which meant they were never coming off the vent, or they were going to be on it for a long, long time."

2. "You got great care. Everyone talks about how people in comas hear everything, but they really respected it. They never did anything without talking to you. They'd say, 'Katie, we're going to suction you now.' They gave great human care—probably the best I've ever seen."

Late that afternoon, my parents arrived from Connecticut, and the first person they saw was my brother, standing by the elevator. They met with the doctor, and together my parents, my brother, and Roy, arranged for my breasts to be pumped (because everyone knew how much I had wanted to nurse my baby) and for Colety to visit me, even though the doctors didn't want this to happen, my family insisted.

My family also recognized that I was in pain from the C-section, and they convinced the doctor, because she started prescribing morphine.

The doctor's notes reflect:

1. ARDS

2. C/Section – Rule out possibility of septic pelvic thrombophlebitis [in which a blood clot from the pelvis has caused sepsis, a systemic infection]

3. Attempting to pump breasts—not very successful, given acute illness

4. Anemia—urine brown—? hemolysis [breakdown of red blood cells]

5. Will allow baby in if OK with ob/peds

I am convinced this last intervention saved my life—that the love from Roy and my family, and most of all the contact with my son—the strong spirit in that tiny body—pulled me back.

Day 5: April 26

Still the fevers persisted, despite the siege of the antibiotics. A cooling blanket was added to the regimen of treatments. My temperature had climbed to 104 degrees, and the white blood cell count, indicating infection, continued to rise. A feeding tube was placed through my nose, into my stomach. Compression stockings were being used on my legs, swollen due to the congestive heart failure, and I was at risk for deep vein thrombosis, or blood clots. A blood thinner, Heparin, was prescribed.

I was deeply sedated. When the Valium, Vecuronium and Versed wore off, I became highly agitated. Yet there was minor improvement in my lungs, and they had been able to lower the volume of oxygen going through the ventilator. And whenever they brought Colety into see me, and laid him on my belly, skin touching skin, my pulse, respiration, and blood pressure went down dramatically. I was soothed.

My sister Chris arrived with her daughter Molly again, and friends came, too, joining Roy, Tom, and my parents. Colety's half-brother and sister, Evan, age twelve, and Kira, fifteen, visited and, gowned, held Colety, his fever gone, for hours. And Roy later told me that he was there for every procedure they did on Colety, even when they weighed him, so that he would not feel abandoned.

The tribe was gathering round Colety and me, sitting vigil by our bedsides.

Day 6: April 27

The doctor's note reads, "Extremely agitated when allowed to wake up. Requiring large amounts of sedation."

The snakes writhe and contract, making whorls in the sand. They have stopped their journey out of the desert. The black crosses on their backs shrink to dots and the light in their trails disappear. The light is gone and they are angry.

Left lower lobe pneumonia was still present, and the cause of the ARDS had yet to be determined. I was fevered, in spite of the cooling blanket. My chest wheezed and crackled when the doctor listened to it. All cultures and stains for specific bacteria were negative. It would remain a mystery what had happened to make me so sick.

Crisis with Colety: Ironically, because he was so well, the hospital decided to discharge him. His fever was gone and he was thriving. The problem was that there was nowhere for him to go, as Roy and my parents were staying at the hospital all day, and at a hotel at night; there was no place to leave a five-day-old baby. The social worker met with my parents, Roy, and my doctor, and they convinced the nursing manager that it was important for "the patient's recovery" (meaning me) that my baby be nearby to visit. They arranged for him to be transferred out of the pediatric intensive care unit (where truly he must have seemed like a giant) to the pediatric ward.

Four angels appear, one for each direction. They gently float down, the air silken. They are the colors of sunset—purples, mauves, pinks, blues. They softly, sweetly float. They are the angels of childbirth, of the babies whose mothers have died when they were born, so the babies are not alone. They watch over children without mothers. The angels touch me as gently as butterflies, brushing their wings against my cheeks. They are real.

Day 7: April 28

The medications were unchanged, my abdomen quite distended, and still there was swelling in my limbs. My lungs were putting out copious secretions—blood and gunk—and they popped and rasped. The fever remained, the x-rays were bad, but the ventilator settings were going down, a good sign. The doctor was concerned that weaning me from the mechanical breathing would be difficult though, due to my agitation. They had tried rousing me, and I had reacted with an unusual pattern—I had started a fast panting: 60 - 80 breaths/minute.

An obstetrician was consulted, and he ordered an ultrasound to rule out abscesses or any post-surgical complications. He also requested a consultation with an Infectious Disease Specialist.

Day 8: April 29

Clinically, everything was the same—the Fever of Unknown Origin cooked along, my lungs rattled and whistled, and I was still sedated with morphine, although Haldol, an anti-psychotic, had replaced the paralyzing agent Versed and the tranquilizing Valium. This change allowed my eyes to open, "sluggishly."

The doctor started me on a steroid, Solumedrol, "with caution," her notes say. Steroids are good when there is inflammation and asthma, but dangerous if there is infection, so it must have been a hard call to make.

The good news was that my abdomen was slightly less distended, my limbs less puffy, and the slow weaning from the ventilator continued. I received a blood transfusion for the hemolytic anemia. And they were bringing my beautiful baby boy to me, allowing skin-to-skin contact, as they placed him on my chest.

He's alive, he's here.

The Infectious Disease Specialist reviewed all the records and examined me. He stated that he:

> Ruled out zoonotic exposure, travel, TB exposure, HIV risk factors, etc. Negative bacterial cultures do not rule out an infectious process such as bacteremia [the presence of bacteria in the blood.] Many pneumonias are culture negative, unfortunately, and endometritis is often a clinical diagnosis without a positive culture ... Most likely, patient's course is explained by post C-section pneumonia, and/or endometritis, leading to sepsis, leading to ARDS.

The pelvic sonogram the obstetrician had ordered came back clear—no signs of infection or abscesses.

My friend Lauren came to visit. Later she told me that when she saw me, I looked asleep, peaceful. She mentioned it to the nurse, who sharply corrected her, saying, "She is a very seriously ill young woman. She may not make it." Lauren was stunned.

She said she told me she wanted to massage my feet, but when she did, she could see, from the bank of monitors above us, that I was getting agitated—my heartbeat, blood pressure and respirations were all rising. She stopped, and instead just talked to me, sitting close to my head, saying, "We are all waiting for you to come back. Your parents are here, and they love you. Roy is here and he loves you, and Colety is here, and he loves you, and he is being taken care of, but we are all waiting for you to come back. You can sleep for as long as you need to, but please come back." As she spoke, my vital signs slowed down; her voice and words calmed me.

Then she went to see Colety. She held him and told him, "Your mommy's here, your mommy loves you, your mommy's going to come back."

Day 9: April 30

A failed extubation, accompanied with severe wheezing, and I got very agitated. My blood pressure soared to 210/130. (Normal for me was 110/70.) I developed increased bronchospasms, sudden constrictions of the muscles in the walls of the bronchioles, deep in the lungs.

I got a dangerous nosebleed when they were placing the tube in my nose for feeding me. It bled so much that they couldn't control it, due to the Heparin (blood thinner) that I was on to prevent blood clots. They packed my nose with gauze and planned to remove it over the next four to five days. Because of the bleeding, they feared the airway had been compromised, so they used the bronchoscope to clear it. They tied my hands to the side of the bed so I wouldn't pull out my tubes or lines.

Due to the low hemocrit (the number of red blood cells in the blood) level, the diagnosis of postpartum hemolytic anemia, and the blood loss from the nosebleed, I received more blood transfusions.

Day 10: May 1

Still I had ARDS, pneumonia, asthma, hemolytic anemia, and post-C-section healing, but was down to only two antibiotics, along with the Solumedrol, Valium, morphine, and Haldol. The catheter and the ventilator remained.

The doctor's note says, "sedated, tries to communicate."

I remember trying to write the word "ice" on a pad, because I couldn't drink and was terribly thirsty, due to the tube down my throat and the fevers. No wonder my visions had me in the desert, with its merciless sun and heat.

My lungs were better, with decreased wheezing, and I had no more edema, or swelling, in my limbs. My white blood cell count was down, and the x-ray showed, for the first time, that the ARDS was resolving. The doctor's plan was to restart the Heparin (she'd discontinued it after the nosebleed) and decrease the steroid. She continued to wean me off the ventilator.

Big news—a lab reported a positive Legionella titer from one of my samples. The information was greeted with caution; the doctor wanted another test, from a more reliable lab, before calling the diagnosis. The medical records don't reflect whether such confirmation ever came, so I could have had Legionnaires' Disease. Breathing in mist or vapor that has been contaminated with the bacteria causes Legionnaires' Disease. According to the CDC, "Hospital buildings have complex water systems, and many people in hospitals already have illnesses that increase their risk for Legionella infection."

Day 11: May 2

The medical chart reported that I was sedated, calm, and able to open my eyes. They did not remove me from the ventilator. No extubation was attempted.

I remained on two antibiotics, Heparin, morphine, Haldol, Valium, and the steroid. Diagnostically, I still had ARDS, asthma, pneumonia, post-partum hemolytic anemia, an increased white blood cell count, and was healing from the Caesarian section. My lungs still wheezed and crackled.

Day 12: May 3

I am awake and I do not understand what is happening. I can see and hear, but I can't talk. I am very hot and thirsty. A nurse comes up and tells me not to try to talk, and then more people surround the bed and I am confused and overwhelmed. I hurt. They tell me to cough, and I cough and gag and they pull and pull and this horrible snaky long thing comes out of my throat. I don't know what has befallen me and I want to know where my baby is. They are taking gauze out of my nose and telling me not to blow my nose, as if that mattered. I am extubated, they tell me.

All I wanted was my baby. My voice was horrid and raspy when I asked for him, due to damage to my larynx from the intubation, a condition that persisted for months.

I was disoriented. Roy was there, and I asked him where the baby was. When he brought our son to me, I felt peace descend and the caress of the angels. Holding Colety in my arms, I gazed into his wise eyes, at last awake for him. I loved him and put him to my breast to nurse. It had been a long journey back to him, but I had made it, grateful for the love and support of my family and friends, and the care of the hospital staff, often given in spite of my opposition. All the light that I had gathered in the desert was for this one precious life, my son's. I had found my baby, and he had found me.

I didn't know what had happened, or what day it was. I didn't know what to believe when Roy explained about the ARDS, the intubation, and how many days I had lost. I was stunned to see my parents there, in the hospital.

I remembered only the C-section, holding my son, and the fever, but not much after that. I recalled wanting to go out to the parking lot and wait for Roy, to get us out of the hospital. But I didn't remember calling my brother, or the intubation, or any of the last ten days, except for the visions I'd had.

Days 13-20:

I spent seven more days in the hospital, recovering from my ordeal, including, according to the doctor's note, "withdrawal from the tremendous amounts of narcotics and benzodiazepines," I had been on. I barely could allow my son out of my arms. I cried a lot, patting my heart.

Chris came, with Molly, and she showed me how to breastfeed. Many of the staff visited me, often late at night when I couldn't sleep, to hear about my visions in the coma. They, too, were in tears, when I spoke about the angels of childbirth, knowing that no motherless child is left unprotected.

The last morning, I spiked another fever, but I did not tell staff. I just needed to get my baby and myself home, blessed home, alive.

My mom stayed with us for about a month to help out, as I was still quite depleted. It took me six more months to recover my strength, as my new doctor explained, "the body cannibalizes itself when it is intubated."

The mystery of why I got ARDS was never definitively solved; the three most likely possibilities are:

1. An amniotic fluid embolism.

2. The stress of the labor and C-section exacerbated an undiagnosed pneumonia, and/or endometritis, into sepsis, which became ARDS

3. Legionnaires' Disease.

Psychological recovery from the trauma and the dissociation has taken years, and I am only now beginning to understand, and only partially, the visions I had while I was in my coma.

Today, my body dances and my lungs breathe deeply. My son thrives: a brilliant, beautiful artist, full of life and light. And I know now, with certainty, that no one dies alone. The angels were with me when I was dying, and then they would have gone to comfort my motherless child. Now, they are with us always, their wings gently caressing our cheeks.

BAHAREH AMIDI

Tomorrow's Poem

I sit carefully aware
I sense the urge or
The desire to write a poem for tomorrow
But what if tomorrow is the last day of my life
In that case I would put down my pen
Walk out and touch the bark of the eucalyptus
And put my ear to earth and listen to my children and my ancestors
I draw a pint of blood and write a poem on the tree trunk
And wait for my ancestor's blessings and my children's cries

What if I Knew

What if I knew that in 2 years' time
It would not be my mother nor I who would die
What if I knew it would be my daughter
For one I would tuck her into bed more often and do an evening prayer
For one I would smell her hair while she was sleeping
and then pretend like I did not lie awake next to her all night long
For one I would let her stay out past her curfew for what is an hour
longer with me when her heart is with the young man she may never
again see
What if I did not imagine such terrible things
but accepted her beauty and her worth
And that is all there is

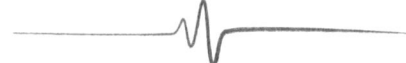

The Size of My Foot Print

Looking at my fingertips
I begin to consider my worth
I realize that at this moment each atom in my body is alive
Feeling the breeze from the desert continents away
Hearing the whisper of the small ant crawling on my knapsack
Being aware of the ulcer the guru carries in his mansion
Aware of the reality of this moment
Every wink of an eye a gift
Every breath a present
Every sigh a new story waiting to be told
The realization that I am the person I was waiting for all along
The right of passage … a truth
and the daisies in the field not yet picked for my grave

DAWN MCGUIRE

Considering Love in a Strip Mall Laundromat

Because he's coughing over his basket, you want to stick around,
watch his back, touch his knobby knuckles, salve the pocks
in his face, balm the runny fissures, fix the gaps in his jacket
with seams like canyon walls, half an inch of orange is
200,000 years—
which is why I could love you.

Him—high heat, long cooling cycle
A raku bowl, clay
burned to a sheen,
sand and fluxes
fused in a frit—
I don't think he needs our help.
Some clean century, even his fragments
will be prized.

ADAM LUXENBERG

Two Deaths and a Lesson

We gathered at the beginning of our second year to discuss our clinical skills class. It was nice to be back at school after a summer break filled with the smell of pine needles under hiking boots and devoid of the odor of old carpet in a windowless room. Clinical skills class was one of my favorite parts of my first year. Most of my school time was spent behind the glow of my computer screen or with a stack of books and papers in front of me, but clinical skills was where I got to interact with people. I was excited to build on my knowledge from the previous year, meet new patients, and progress as a medical student. But I was hesitant to make the call to one person from my first year of medical school whom I would be continuing to get to know during my second year. My elder mentor, Glenn.

I typed his name into the Google search window. Remembering how his health was declining in the course of our final visits, I had a feeling that he might have died over the summer. As I typed, Google began to automatically complete the search. It finished Glenn's last name and added the word legacy. The results that followed included his legacy.com website and obituaries in various newspapers. The otherwise innocuous autocomplete seemed like the most insensitive innovation.

Glenn wasn't just the healthy, engaging, 92-year-old I thought he would be when I met him. Although he was those things, he also became more than that. I visited with him only two times before he died, but those visits changed the way I experienced my grandfather's death that came only a few months after I learned about his. Before I met Glenn most people I knew who were his age were relatives. Our relationship began because I was paired with him in a program intended to deconstruct barriers between medical students and elders. We called our matches "elder mentors," but I don't know if "mentor" is really the right word for the relationship that developed between Glenn and me.

When I knocked on Glenn's door at the retirement community I found the person I expected him to be. He was a talkative, healthy-looking elder and exactly the kind of person I imagined that this program would choose for us. As he sat before me, very upright in a recliner that begged him to do otherwise, he told me stories about his life in an era that I know only though books and movies.

"I was a pilot with Pan Am," Glenn said. "I helped develop their 747 program and flew Pacific routes out of LA for most of my career."

Glenn conducted himself like a pilot. His apartment at the top of the building gave him a view over the entire Bay Area that suited the way he seemed to oversee his surroundings just as if he were scanning a runway before takeoff. In the bright room I seemed to be only one of the many objects in his constantly scanning gaze. Glenn and I talked about his childhood in Berkeley, how he found himself working in the Pan Am offices on Treasure Island, and how that led to a pilot's seat on flying boats making trips to Hawaii. Glenn had been all over the world during the last century. His knowledge and life experience were vast.

Although Glenn's life experiences were diverse and spanned the course of almost a century, they didn't include many health problems. He was very proud to tell me that he had been to the hospital only twice—once to have his tonsils removed, and once again about ten years before we met to have a stent placed.

"I'm really fortunate to be so healthy. A lot of people around here have to deal with so much nonsense with their doctors and insurance," he said, chuckling. Glenn was proud to be able to say that he was so healthy, especially since he lived among people who weren't always as fortunate.

As he told me that he was feeling older than he had ever felt before, he became more serious. He told me about how many of his friends declined from good health to illness very quickly. But he was uncomfortable discussing health problems. It seemed that he had identified with being healthy for so long, it was hard for him to see people around him, with whom he had so much in common, getting sick.

Many of the interactions I had with people during my first year of medical school were about their health concerns and took place in doctor's offices. With Glenn it was nice to get to know someone I wouldn't normally meet, without focusing on problems in his life. We talked about things that I would talk about with my own friends. He was very aware of current technology and thought many of the things that I take for granted were absolutely amazing. We talked about our families, and shared family stories. When the conversation turned to activities that we enjoyed, we found that we both loved hiking and Glenn told me about his trips to national parks and the advocacy work that he and his wife did on behalf of open space preserves. Although Glenn and I met only because of this program, I felt that he was somebody I would have enjoyed getting to know in any circumstance. Our developing friendship didn't seem forced or any more difficult to establish than it would have been had we been closer in age.

After a few hours of talking I made plans with Glenn to meet again in a few months. When I left Glenn's apartment I began thinking about other people in my life with whom I would like to spend time and whom I'd like to get to know in the way that I had started to get to know Glenn. Since Glenn reminded me of my grandparents, I thought about my relationships with all four of my grandparents.

I'm lucky that all of my grandparents have been actively involved in my life. When I met Glenn I didn't know many other people my age whose grandparents were all alive. He made me want to sit in a room with my grandparents and absorb their stories. I was paired with him as a way to try to break barriers between people my own age and people Glenn's age and I wanted to do the same with the people who were already important in my life. Of course I knew all of my grandparents much better than I knew Glenn after having talked to him one time for a couple of hours. However, in those few hours I was able to talk to him in a way that I was never really able to talk to my grandparents. The conversation I had with him was much more natural than with them. I wanted to become friends with my grandparents in the way that I had started to become friends with Glenn. I felt guilty that this had never really crossed my mind before my visit with him. My grandparents were not exactly my friends—just my grandparents. I was motivated to get to know my grandparents on a different level.

The next time I saw Glenn I was excited to tell him about all of the things that had happened in my life since the last time we met. I had begun to learn how to conduct physical exams, I knew how to ask people questions about their medical history, and had become close friends with my classmates. I wanted to share all of this with him. When we began to talk I realized that far more had happened in Glenn's life since our last meeting. Over the course of the three months that had gone by he had been hospitalized two times for a week each time. He looked different from the last time I had seen him. He sat in the same chair, but this time the chair seemed to be pulling him in exactly the way it failed to the last time I was with him. He didn't really look around the room, he just looked at me or stared off into the distance with far less command of his surroundings. It seemed as if the alertness that had so distinguished Glenn the first time I met him was diminished this time. He just didn't look well.

Glenn told me he didn't feel well, either. He was hospitalized the first time because he had fainted while walking with his wife. He was rushed to the emergency room and was subsequently admitted to the hospital. He said it was a really scary experience to be taken to the hospital. After all, this was really his first experience with the full face of the medical system. He said something that I've heard many times in my short experience as a medical student: that people at the hospital didn't really spend a lot of time paying attention to him. He said that except for a few nice doctors and nurses he didn't think anybody really cared that he was there. People were coming in and out of his room, telling him to do things, giving him food, changing medicines, and it was all so jarring.

When Glenn was discharged from the hospital he was sent home with a slew of new medications and directions to make appointments with his cardiologist to sort out an arrhythmia that was newly diagnosed. A month went by before he found himself in the hospital a second time. This hospitalization happened the same way the first one did. He felt faint, lost his balance, and the next thing he knew, he was on his way to the emergency room. He said the second time in the hospital was less jarring, but still scary. This time it was scarier because he realized that he was becoming one of the sick people he had prided himself on not being before these incidents.

Glenn had gone from being very healthy, or at least appearing very healthy, to being very ill over only a few months. The same few months that felt like a few days to me had felt like years for him. He told me that the combination of doctors' visits, an increased daily medicine routine, and not feeling well had made him feel as though he wasn't in control of anything. He spoke about dying at this meeting, something he hadn't done at the last.

Instead of treating me like a friend this time, Glenn wanted me to assume the role of a medical professional. He wanted me to help him understand some of the medical aspects of what was happening to him. He wanted to know if everyone experiences hospitals the way he had, and if making doctor's appointments, going to doctor's appointments, and filling prescriptions felt like a full-time job to everyone. I just didn't have the answers, nor did I want to have the answers. Our second meeting felt much more like the encounters I had had with patients regularly in my clinical skills class. The first time I met with Glenn he felt like a friend that I had made outside of the medical world. The second time we met, he was a patient.

I still enjoyed being with him that second time, but in a different way than I had the first time. Seeing his health change so quickly, and realizing how different our encounter was once he didn't feel well gave new urgency to the feelings that I had about wanting to connect with my grandparents. My second meeting was right before my summer break and I hoped that fewer school responsibilities would give me the time to engage with my grandparents, and it did. I went out to dinner with my grandparents more often, I made an effort to stop by their house and just talk to them, I called my grandparents who live far away a few times a month. I made an effort to have the same experience that I had with Glenn with my grandparents.

Much like Glenn, my grandfather had been very healthy his entire life. Unlike Glenn, I don't think my grandfather had ever been a patient at a hospital. As a doctor he didn't seem to have a lot of confidence in the medical system when it came to his own health. He liked to stick to the doctoring side of things and luckily he was able to do this for most of his life.

My grandfather's decline began in the same manner as Glenn's. The first event came out of nowhere and the whole trip from health to death happened very quickly. One night, while my grandparents were on vacation, he passed out after dinner. He came to a few minutes later, but refused to go the emergency room. After a lot of pleading he finally went to the emergency room, but the doctors couldn't figure out what had caused him to lose consciousness with any certainty. My grandfather didn't think there was anything to worry about, just the combination of a big meal and maybe too high a dose of his blood pressure medication. That event was the first time that anyone in my family feared that something was really wrong with my grandfather's health. It also was the event that made it clear to the family that my grandfather didn't have much interest in becoming a patient, even as his health declined.

The next few months were difficult for everyone in my family. My grandfather went from a self-sufficient and fairly healthy man to his death. Because of his wishes all my family could do was watch the decline happen. Soon after my grandfather's passing out episode he developed pneumonia. Around this time a preexisting problem with swallowing food was exacerbated, and he lost a significant amount of weight from the combination of eating very little and fighting pneumonia. During all of this he still refused to be seen by a physician. He would consult with some of his old colleagues who were still in practice, but he never entered the medical system the way one would expect a person with my grandfather's problems to do.

Although my grandfather's body was failing him, he was still the same person he had always been mentally, and I was able to visit him many times. It had been a little more than a year since Glenn's death, and my experience seeing him sick was a constant reminder of how I wanted these last visits with my grandfather to be meaningful. When I visited with him he had trouble talking and moving around on the couch where he would sit all day, but our conversations were fairly normal. He was mentally engaged, and that made me less troubled by the fact that these visits were very likely our last interactions. Through all of my grandfather's health problems, his mental alertness was important to me. I never worried that he was doing anything that he didn't want to be doing, or that he wasn't getting treatment because he didn't know what was available. He was in charge of everything all the way up until the night he died.

My grandfather died at home four months after the episode when he passed out while on vacation. My parents live only a few minutes away from my grandparents, but the night my grandfather died they were out of town. I made my way over to the house when I found out my grandfather had died. When I got there I sat on the couch in my grandparents' living room with my aunt and my grandmother into the early hours of the morning waiting for the people from the mortuary to come take his body.

"He was always the captain of the ship, even until the end," my grandma said, lovingly, making a reference to my grandpa's passion for sailing.

I saw my grandma in a way that I had never seen her before. She was experiencing the first moments of life without a man with whom she had spent her whole adult life. She was calm, and spent the time talking about memories of my grandfather that came popping into her mind. The memories she began telling represented some of the highlights of all those years. Just as I had felt Glenn treated me like a peer that first day we had met, I felt as though my grandmother was treating me as a peer while we sat together on the couch.

When my grandfather became ill, and then when he died, I had many thoughts about meeting Glenn. Meeting him and seeing his decline and death helped me cope with my grandfather's. Without Glenn I don't think I would have been able to appreciate those last few months that I had with my grandfather while he was healthy. I also don't think that I would have taken his initial illness so seriously and been so worried about finding time to have the visits with him that ended up being the last ones we had.

Meeting Glenn was an experience that I had because of medical school. Although I have learned a lot about medicine, and how to begin to assume the role of a physician, I have also learned about life outside of the world of medicine. I didn't want to lose Glenn this year, and I really didn't want to lose my grandfather. Learning how to become a doctor has been important, but those lessons would be less instructive if medical school hadn't also taught me about how to deal with normal life as well.

JULIANNA WATERS

Jim's Prescription

Have I shown you the pills? he asked.
He turned around,
desk chair squeaked and swiveled,
grabbed a white bag off the credenza,
placed the bag between us on his desk,
grim from effort,
skin like tissue.
Go ahead, he said,
take them out.
I opened it,
thin lips of paper parted,
my touch light.
I reached in, lifted
the plastic bottle from inside,
held it in my hand.
Here they are, I said.
Here they are, he echoed.
We looked down at the bottle
as if it were a world wonder,
an amber chasm,
my eyes wide,
his half open,
red rimmed and blue.
Let's open it, he whispered.
Let's, I said, and twisted the lid.

We peered in like children,
stared as if we'd found a goldfish bowl
full of yellow and white striped submarines.
They look like bees, he said.
They look like bricks, I said.
Bricks?
Bricks. Bricks to build a bridge with.
He nodded his head,
adjusted his oxygen, said,
Let's spill them out.
He tilted the bottle,
poured the pills onto a sheet of paper.
We have to open every capsule, he said,
pour the powder into a milkshake,
juice, something.
He looked at me,
face gaunt and flushed,
hair cropped close and silver.
Would you mind helping?
No, I said,
heart like a drum,
No, I wouldn't mind.
Maybe next week? he asked.
Yes, next week.
I looked at my lap.
I love you, he said.
I love you, too.
You can't be there, he said
(to his fingernails)
(to the the jade turtle on his desk)
I wish you could, he said, sighed,
rubbed his hand across the fuzz on his head.
Have I told you about driving through Nevada? he asked,
top down at dawn?
Tell me again, I said.
Tell me again.

MOLLY GILES

Odds on Ends

Most novels end badly. I'm not talking about mysteries, which usually satisfy, and which I never read, I'm talking about literary novels. Most of them should be left on the airplane right next to the puke bag about two thirds through. Surely the enduring charm of books like *Remembrance of Things Past* and *Finnegan's Wake* is that so few readers finish them. Thus they remain chronic works in progress. The best thing about *Finnegan's Wake* of course is that you can pretend to have finished it because the last line snakes so craftily into the first. It is a beautiful last line: "a way a lone a last a loved a long the … " and it made me think of the (very few) other last lines that I have admired over the years.

"They lived happily ever after"—who can knock that? Certainly not Henry Green, who used it as the last line in his lovely novella, *Loving*. Another childhood favorite—"And it was still hot!"—Max, returning from his rumpus with the Wild Things, finds supper waiting and so ends his adventures with a satisfactory meal. Ludwig Bemelmans' *Madeline* ends, like many children's books do, with a lullaby: "And now goodnight, said Miss Clavell. And she turned out the light. And closed the door. And that's all there is, there isn't any more."

When I think how many books and student stories especially start with a character waking up, the idea of ending with a character going safely to sleep is not unappealing. Or perhaps safe, but not safe in bed. Many books crash land their heroes—I'm thinking of *Moby Dick*, when Ishmael is picked up from the wreckage of the *Pequod*. Or the delightful end of

Joseph Heller's *Catch-22*: "The knife came down, missing him by inches, and he took off."

Some writers go ahead and stick the knife in. The death of a main character is terminal closure for most pieces of fiction, though many books, like *Anna Karenina* and *Emma Bovary*, soldier on long after their heroines have disappeared, to their detriment I might add. When I think of books that end with an actual death, I remember the gorgeously grisly "and then they were upon her," from Shirley Jackson's "The Lottery." "The Delicate Prey," by Paul Bowles ends with a nomad buried up to his neck in the sand, singing "through the cold hours for the sun that would bring first warmth, then heat, thirst, fire, visions. The next night he did not know where he was, did not feel the cold. The wind blew dust along the ground into his mouth as he sang." The young traveler dying of dysentery in the middle of the Indian Ocean in Jeffrey Eugenides' story "Airmail" wants to send a final letter to his family "but soon he realized that there was nothing left of him to do it—nothing at all—no person left to hold a pen or to send word to the people he loved, who would never understand."

Margaret Atwood's short story "Happy Endings" features two characters, John and Mary, who meet and marry, or don't, in version after version. "You'll have to face it," Atwood writes finally, "the endings are the same however you slice it … The only authentic ending is the one provided here: *John and Mary die. John and Mary die. John and Mary die.*" My own favorite death line comes from a story my daughter wrote when she was eight: "And Jenny never got out of that attic alive."

Death by itself of course does not do the trick. We readers want our evil characters punished before they go and our good guys redeemed. Sidney Carton's famous speech from the gallows in *Tale of Two Cities* manages to rise above his own demise: "It is a far, far better thing that I do, than I have ever done; it is a far, far better rest that I go to than I have ever known."

Some authors stop short of killing their characters and settle for doing as much damage as they can, presumably for the character's own good. Flannery O'Connor and Annie Proulx are ruthless character assassins, and there is no doubt they enjoy it, there is girlish laughter in many of their ends and no small amount of sadism. Here is little snob Julian after his embarrassingly fat mother has dropped dead on the street in O'Connor's "Everything that Rises Must Converge." "'Help, help!' he shouted, but his voice was thin, scarcely a thread of sound. The lights drifted farther away the faster he ran and his feet moved numbly as if they carried him nowhere. The tide of darkness seemed to sweep him back to her, postponing from moment to moment his entry into the world of guilt and sorrow."

One of my favorite ends—well, one of my favorite stories—Frank O'Connor's "Guests of the Nation"—again ushers a fairly innocent character into the world of guilt and sorrow from which he will never recover. A young Irish soldier, he has just executed the two English prisoners he had befriended and after their deaths he stands outside and looks up at the sky: "and the birds and the bloody stars were all far away, and I was somehow very small and very lost and lonely like a child astray in the snow. And anything that happened to me afterwards, I never felt the same about again." This last line, which O'Connor wrote and rewrote, is a blunt telling, almost a diagram of epiphany, and it has been echoed in stories since. You will hear it clearly if less elegantly in the last line of John Updike's "The A&P" after the young grocery clerk has quit his job and says, "My stomach kind of fell as I felt how hard the world was going to be to me hereafter."

Sometimes the hardness of the world is a relief. In William Trevor's story "The Room," a wife realizes she is going to leave a husband she loves but can no longer live with. Trevor's wording, as always, is elegantly elegiac: "Katherine turned to walk back the way she'd come. It wouldn't be a shock, nor even a surprise. He expected no more of her than what she'd given him, and she would choose her moment to say that she must go. He would understand; she would not have to tell him. The best that love could do was not enough, and he would know that also."

Stories like the above torque the character into change in the very last lines. A famous example is Joyce's "Araby" and this is a line I do not love. After a boy's dreams of chivalrous romance are shattered, he says:

"… I saw myself as a creature driven and derided by vanity; and my eyes burned with anguish and anger." My dislike of this line stems not from Joyce but from the English Lit teachers whom I hold responsible for the hundreds of undergraduate stories I have since read which end with a young man or woman howling over heartbreak at midnight, usually drunk outside a fraternity house, before throwing up.

I prefer endings that go out with a whimper, not a bang. "Ah Bartleby! Ah humanity!" is a big soulful sigh that embraces the whole world and that works for me. So does "The horror. The horror." So does the end of *The Great Gatsby* with all those little boats beating out to sea. But these are tricky ends for us lesser writers to emulate, tipped toward the disaster of satire as they are, and I'd advise against attempting them. We lesser writers however need not worry. We have lots to choose from.

There are joke endings, which of course work better for short stories than for novels, as the story form itself is close to the joke: "A woman is sitting in her old shuttered house. She knows that she is alone in the whole world; every other thing is dead. The doorbell rings" (Thomas Bailey Aldrich) and surprise endings—"The Gift of the Magi"—and ironical endings like "Hills Like White Elephants": "I feel fine," she said. "There's nothing wrong with me. I feel fine"—and lyrical endings, like the last lines of "The Dead": "His soul swooned slowly as he heard the snow falling faintly through the universe, and faintly falling, like the descent of their last end, upon all the living and the dead." (We would tear that apart in a workshop—too many adverbs, too much alliteration.) There are surreal endings—John Cheever does these superbly, when his narrative simply takes leave of the world of everyday and with no fanfare enters the world of ancient myth: "The sea that morning was iridescent and dark. My wife and my sister were swimming—Diana and Helen—and I saw their uncovered heads black and gold in the dark water. I saw them come out and I saw that they were naked, unshy, beautiful, and full of grace, and I watched naked women walk out of the sea." There are seeded endings, like the marvelous implosion of Tobias Wolff's "Bullet in the Brain," when the narrator dies to the memory a childhood softball game and his wonder at the overheard words: "Short's the best position they is."

There are pitch-perfect character endings, as in *The Age of Innocence*, when Edith Wharton's hero cannot meet the love of his life, much as we want him to, or when Evan Connell's *Mrs. Bridge* finds herself wedged in her garage, unable to get out. There are symmetrical endings, like John LeCarre's *Spy Who Came In From the Cold*, which begins and ends with a death at the Berlin Wall. There are endings which resolve the character's present dilemma and give them a shove toward their future. Huck Finn lights out for the Territory. The stoic widow in Bharti Mukherjee's "The Management of Grief" lights out for a different kind of territory. "I do not know where this voyage I have begun will end. I do not know which direction I will take. I dropped the package on a park bench and started walking."

Just getting your character up and out the door is often enough and stories that end with an action that steps toward the future almost always work. Many stories do end with walking, the overused word "home," and the word "tomorrow." Perhaps the most famous last line, in American fiction at least, comes at the end of *Gone With the Wind*, when Scarlett O'Hara, having lost Rhett Butler, decides that "Tomorrow, I'll think of some way to get him back. After all, tomorrow is another day."

So thinking of our own work, let's take some other tips from these writers: Margaret Mitchell actually wrote the last scene of *Gone With the Wind* first, and "Tomorrow is Another Day" was one of her original choices for the title. Of course, "Tote the Weary Load" was too. But if you can do what she did, and write your last scene first, the rest of your book or story should flow toward it inevitably. You will be a lucky writer if you know your story's end. If you don't know it specifically, you do probably know from the start whether you are writing a comedy or a tragedy, whether your piece is going to end with a marriage and a party or a death and a funeral, but you may not have actually visualized it. If you can, do so. Write it down. If you can't, take comfort from these words from Ernest Gaines; he said that every time he sits down to write a book all he knows is that he's on a train and he's "going to Georgia." He doesn't know who is going to sit next to him or what route the train is going to take but he is sure of his destination. Who knows what Georgia means to Ernest Gaines!

He lives in Louisiana. But if you can fix your own Georgia On Your Mind you'll at least be headed in the right direction. Take your time. Enjoy the trip.

Some other suggestions:

Mirror-image your scenes, so instead of writing your last scene first try turning your first scene upside down and making it your last. This seems to me a neat little trick when it works, as it does so beautifully in the LeCarre book with two deaths at the Berlin Wall bookending the narrative.

Think circularly. We are told that plot is linear—conflict leading to crisis leading to resolution—but the perfect geometry for plot is actually the circle. When you think about it, no closure is as satisfying as that which comes full circle. I have just finished reading a friend's novel manuscript; the book starts out strong, with a boy seeing the same monster his delusional father hallucinates; it goes on to describe the next thirty years of the boy's life but never again mentions the monster or the boy's uncanny ability to see as others do. As a result, the end peters out, needlessly, because with just a touch here and there woven through and with a final twist of vision—he either sees the monster again, or, better, can see the world his own way now and so sees nothing—the entire book will work.

And on work, why not let real life do the work for you? As a judge for the PEN/Faulkner fiction contest last winter, I read almost 400 books published in 2007 and one of the things that struck me was how many of the novels were based on real people. I read about Frank Lloyd Wright, William Blake, Edward Curtis, Edward Steichen, Woody Guthrie, Isaac Babel, Commodore Perry, Florence Nightingale, and Hitler, among others, and in fact one of the winners of the contest, David Leavitt's *The Indian Clerk*, was a richly imagined account of an uneducated real-life mathematical genius, who came from poverty in Madras to dazzle the established dons at Cambridge in 1913.

These historical novels all had exhaustive pages of acknowledgements and were as well-researched as biographies. It was clear the authors had worked like beavers. But I was puzzled. Why use an-already-lived-life for your novel instead of a made-up one? And then it occurred to me. It was because the authors knew the end. They knew how Frank Lloyd Wright's love affair panned out and how Steichen's divorce had ended and how Woody Guthrie had died. One of the biggest problems every writer faces in story telling—THE END—had been solved, not by imagination, but by history.

If you don't like history, try poetry. Aim for a beautiful ending. Don't fear beauty. We want to be moved when we finish a book. Beauty—remember the end of "The Dead"—moves us, so does loss, so does love, so does any genuine emotion. Because we recoil from sentimentality (or think we do, I'm not sure that's ever been true) we also sometimes recoil from feeling. I like an end that makes me feel—makes me laugh or breaks my heart or just makes me put the book down and stare out the window. I like a little burst of lyricism. When you have come to your end, read your final passage out loud. Do you sniffle, pat your heart, and think God, I am brilliant? Good. If your end has come from genuine gratitude or genuine grief, keep it. If you feel even a twitch of shame, get rid of the part that shames you, the lie that's somewhere buried in the words. You know it's there. Kill it.

This by the way is why I think we say that writing can't be taught. So much of it is based on the body's physical response. If you don't feel that sick twitch of shame, even when the sentimental or manipulative is pointed out to you, no one can teach it to you. This doesn't mean your work won't sell or be popular. It just means it won't be any good. If you don't hear that little "click" when the end snaps into place no one can teach that to you either. You have to listen with the patience of a safecracker, turning the words over and over in every sentence until—and there is no other way for me to describe it—you hear "click" and the treasure box opens.

If you remain unimpressed with yourself, don't be discouraged, just rewrite. I mentioned that "Guests of the Nation" was one of my favorite stories—Frank O'Connor rewrote the last line many many times. John Fowles was an obsessive rewriter, even after his books were published. You may have to struggle with a truckload of revisions. Do it. What else do you have to do with your life?

If after countless revisions of the final scene, you still don't have it, there's something wrong in the middle. You may have written past your end. Go back a few pages. Have you said too much? Gone on too long? You may have the right last line on page 12 of a 15-page story but not the last scene; pull the line out and hold on to it. Another good bet is to go back to about the ¾ mark of your manuscript. This is where most books bog down. You may have taken a wrong turn in there somewhere. Maybe added an extra character or plot twist, or, more likely, left out something important.

Ask yourself: *Did you leave the key scene out?* This is the single most common problem of unpublished novels. The author may have that key scene in his or her head but it's not on the page yet.

Another idea is to scuffle around in the scenes of your book or story and look for some little object that can carry the ending, the orphan's locket, the deed to the ruby mine, some *thing*, preferably not a gun (the minute a gun comes into most student stories, characterization goes out the window), but something tangible to point toward the end. "The appropriate object is always at hand," foxy Ezra Pound said, and if you look in your story you will see that he is right. There is something in there you haven't used yet. Ann Beattie centered her much anthologized story "Janus" around a decorative bowl and she ends with her character gazing at it: "… Alone in the living room at night, she often looked at the bowl sitting on the table still and safe, unilluminated. In its way, it was perfect: the world cut in half, deep and smoothly empty. Near the rim, even in dim light, the eye moved toward one small flash of blue, a vanishing point on the horizon."

Some stories, like the Tobias Wolff story mentioned above, end with a step back; the character regresses to a happier time. The end of *Pulp Fiction* uses this technique; after all the bloodshed we are allowed to enjoy the characters in action once more. If your character is stuck in some tragic situation and you want to extricate him, try using a jump forward; project him or her into the future. You will have to change tense to do this.

Raymond Carver shows you how in "Where I'm Calling From": He leaves his character at the payphone at the rehab center about to call first his wife and then his girlfriend: To his wife: "I won't bring up business," he says. "I won't raise my voice." And to his girlfriend: "'Hello sugar,' I'll say when she answers. 'It's me.'"

Another suggestion: Meditate. Sounds like old new age, but works. If you've been banging your head against a wall and there still is no hole in that wall, take twenty minutes, hunker down somewhere, preferably low to the ground with your back to your desk, and go gratefully receptively blank. See what comes to you. It may not be the right thing. That's okay. Write it down and meditate again tomorrow.

Keep a dream journal. Ask for guidance while you sleep.

Be attentive to any ideas that come to you in the shower, driving over bridges, climbing stairs, walking, running or swimming. Ideas like to come when we're on the move, far from pen and paper. As we work on our work, ideas and phrases come by themselves; you'll overhear the checker in the market say the one perfect thing you need. Stay open. Find a stick and write on the sand. Jam out forty different endings, each one crazier than the rest. Don't throw any of them away. Well. Throw a few of them away. Throw away "And then I woke up." Throw away "Somewhere a dog barked. Another dog answered." Throw away anything in italics. Don't be deliberately ambiguous in the hopes that your readers will understand something you do not. But don't lose faith. Remember that you do not have to solve the entire world. Just this one little piece of stupid prose. You don't have to figure everything out. Who could? We are not all that smart, we writers. Most of us don't know that much more at the end of our lives than we did at the beginning. Often, thanks to various forms of senile dementia, we know less. Most people's last words are probably, "Oh shit." I can't think of a single book that ends with those two words.

Fiction is supposed to be less shitty than life. It is supposed to make more sense than life. That's one of the reasons we read, one of the reasons we write. We want to feel we are forgiven and that there is hope, and the ending of choice in today's fiction is the ending that offers both.

Redemption is and always has been a staple of American fiction and—not to sound too cynical—it is marketable. A good end—when it works— when it transcends the material, literally leaves the page, transfers to the reader, and expands, embracing the universe, as in "The Dead," is a very good end—and when it fails, well, give it another shot and if it continues to fail, the hell with it. As has been famously said, No book is ever finished, it is simply abandoned. Preferably abandoned thirty pages before the end, face down, on the plane.

MARTHA LUNNEY

Push!
a doula for Zenobia

Someone left the windows open all night *again* and this morning even the pigeons had to be shooed outside. The radiators bang and hiss a syncopated beat and the sunlight, between showers, brightens the blue carpet and suffuses the room with a promise of warmth. Zenobia is punctual and knocks lightly at the door before entering. She is tall, dark-skinned, a few years older than I, and most days offers me an expectant look as she seats herself that relays her perception of the power dynamic between us. Though still an intern, I am, in her eyes, the professional. She is a woman from the projects whose return home each day after work is a path among addicts, the homeless and hookers. There is something meek about her, even shy, though I remember that she's held her own against more than one would-be mugger.

Most of each session we talk. At the end of the hour, for the last five or ten minutes, Zenobia sits in silence, eyes downcast. I never interrupt this quiet. When our time is up, she nods to herself, as if she has internalized what she needs from our talk, has let it take root inside and is ready to leave. Today Zenobia looks hesitant and then says she's thinking of dropping out of the journalism classes that she only just enrolled in. "Writing's my baby," she confesses and reaches for the Kleenex. "I can't expose it to a room of strangers. I just don't think I can do this." She is looking at me with large, green eyes brimming with tears. I love this woman—and I can't let her back away from this step. My instinct tells me to push. Looking at her now, leaning toward me in her chair, I know she is full of yearning and disappointment and fear. "Writing is my *baby*," she says again pleadingly.

"That's right, it is," I tell her. "It *is* your baby. And do you know what you go through to get that baby born?" I am praying to myself as I speak to her, charged with feeling, *'she has come so far; please ...'* "After months of your body growing this new life inside, at some point your water breaks and then there's crap all over the floor—and it can happen anywhere and it's messy and embarrassing. No one tells you about *that*. But you go through a cataclysm to get that baby born. You endure contractions that feel like they could split you in two. Sometimes you want to beg, against all that's rational, for someone to literally stop the clock because you don't think you can go forward another second." The tattoo of another rain shower on the windows accompanies the clanging of the radiator pipes in an entrancing crescendo that is filling the room. Now I, too, lean forward in my chair.

"Even after pleading for the pain to stop, when your genitalia's swollen and distended like a ring of mountaintops, raised by tectonic forces inside, you push and push until you're dripping with sweat and sounds come from you that only an animal would make, so you thought. You rip off your shirt because you feel like a furnace—disdaining, finally, the niceties of everyday life. And when you're convinced that not even the person who loves you best can turn back the clock and make you un-pregnant, that there's only one way through this, you reach deep into the magma of your being, where you never knew you could reach before and, through *sheer determination*, you push and you push until finally you've done it: that baby you've loved since you first conceived it slips out like a fish and is caught in the expectant hands of your doula. And you are flashing through exhaustion, euphoria, a hormonal rainstorm, effusing so much love for this life you created, this journey you undertook—. You're right. It *is* your baby." I sit back in my chair. She stares at me slack-jawed. The radiator is quiet. She will sit a long time in silence today.

FRAN BRAHMI

Hydrangeas

A heaviness dissipates
flatness animates
and darkness lightens
in shades of grey.
Hydrangeas
in the summer heat
easily revived
by cool droplets
of unexpected rain,
bowed heads rise.

As she lay dying

As she lay dying
I colored mandalas.
Is she in pain
or sweetly sleeping?
Curled onto herself
she lies on the beige sofa
her breath
labored and shallow
mouth agape.
As she lay dying
I colored mandalas.
Remembering
who she once was:
fuchsia, green, and goldenrod.
As she lay dying
I colored mandalas.

Night Rounds

Amid the chatter
and the charts
the buzzing and the beeping
Listen to the humming
silent steps
Find the
Forgotten.

PTSD
She never spoke of it
It spoke to her
She had no words for it
Just an emptiness
A hollow where she hid it.

WENDY PATRICE-WILLIAMS

My Mother's Ears

Why tell you about my mother's ears? Because I need to tell the story. Because I want to learn something. Because it haunts me. I don't want to tell it the same old tired way—parroting my mother's words. It's not that her story isn't valid. It's that I have my own story and hers never changed.

It's a story of listening, listening, listening until my ears closed; a story of repeating words so she could hear me: "Canned Peas!" (not "vasoline"); "Valentine!" (not "happy time"); "Fruit Cocktail!" (not "soup 'n ale"). It's a story about me finding my own voice, listening inside for my own version.

It's a story of a woman distressed over a hearing loss that stole her career dream: court reporting. The story of one accustomed to loss. And it's a story about a little girl, now an adult, who can tell the story any way she wishes, even differently than her MFA program told her to.

The story of ears. My ears. My mother's ears. What's said and what's not said. A cacophony of sounds. Mom called what she heard "bells." Her ears full of wild sound and sometimes, she described it in a fun way: "You should hear'em, Wend. All kinds of bells—loud bells, soft bells, harsh bell. Buzzes, rings, screeches—every kind of sound." "Tintinabulation" is the word that I thought must describe it when I first read Poe's poem.

Mom seemed, much of the time, in her own world, washing dishes at the sink, radio program blathering, blabbering, a commotion of mumbles. Sounds that protected her, too, from my curses, "swear words," my aunt called them once when I spoke to Mom "under my breath."

The beach towel where my mother sat on her lawn chair at the ocean was an island unto itself. She loved to read under the umbrella as my brother and I played in the waves. Would she have heard me had I yelled? Would she know I needed help? Once I got flounced by a wave and caught under the rope marking off the swim area. Sand, bubbles, light, dark, the world swirling in circles until I sat coughing in the sand, the water sucking at my legs trying to pull me into the undertow.

She was in her own world at home, too, digging, fertilizing, planting, weeding. I could be behind her but she wouldn't know. She wouldn't say, for instance, "That you, Wend?" She was an imperturbable presence, a ghost, a different sort of person with bells clanging in her ears. A person who did not want to go to the movies or to concerts or to meetings because it was simply "too damn hard to hear."

She was a stay-at-home mom until I was eleven and my brother fourteen. Neighbors talked to her and she talked to me. So many stories I don't want to tell. I've told them before, purged them, flushed them out of my system—stories of hate and fear, bitterness and disappointment, sadness, fury, agony, terror, abuse, rage, destruction, loneliness, betrayal, abandonment. People leaving each other—a family pattern, a family pastime as natural as swimming in summer or a mother nursing a baby. I don't want to write that story either about the boys pinching my cunt under the chlorinated water of Linden Pool while my mother read her book on the makeshift beach beyond the chain link fence.

I want to tell you how my mother made lifelong friends of her audiologist, Marvin Kline, and his assistant, Suzie O'Donnell. How my mother baked them Christmas shortbread cookies with multi-colored sprinkles and brought each a red holiday stocking of fudge though both were Jewish. How they loved her, sympathized with her, cared for her when she needed them, hearing aid on the fritz. How they took her right away, how she sat in the seat for the hearing test like a pilot of an airplane. She wore headphones and held a joystick. Her chair swiveled as she reported her truth in short bursts: "No," "Yes," "Low," High," "Shrill," "Dull." How they listened to her, heard her, provided for her, served her for over fifty years—my mother's champions, giving her access to a world beyond the clicks and tones, buzzes and ticks, clangs and bongs.

And I want to tell you about her perfect silence there under the mountain ash tree, there beside the roses, trowel in hand and seedlings, there in the shade, kneeling on the lawn, there wearing her lime green pedal pushers and sleeveless shirt to match with red trim around the arm holes. There in nature, she had her autonomy, integrity, grace. There my mother was glorious—smelling the warm humus, plumping up the dark soil around a newly planted stem. Her rhododendrons, her tulips. Her rose bushes, her blue bells. Her horse chestnut and mountain ash and pine tree. Her holly trees—beloved red berries and prickly leaves—prizes that strangers stopped for around the Christmas holiday, asking for a cut, and she was more than generous, delivering branches to this one on Crann Street and that one on Fitzpatrick and that one on Chestnut. One for the mailman, the milkman, the gas man.

There was a peacefulness inside her despite the noise, is this what I'm trying to say among my tears? And why cry? She suffered and I knew this. Her soft pupils though told of a rich inner life. This part, she withheld from us. A part beyond the complaints, bitterness, and tenth car credo (*If ten cars line up at the red light, you can be damn sure that tenth car—the one that won't make it through green—is us*). A peacefulness was inside her that she could access. Was it her love of nature that gave her those eyes? Her love of Norse stories she'd read as a child so her imagination was big? The poetry she wrote as a teen? (*A faint haze, A growing darkness; Man's cultivation, And lo! a moustache.*) Was it hiking at Greenwood Lake summers, the walks she took with her Aunt Haddy, the botanist, identifying plants and wildflowers? Was it hearing the tiny waves tapping the lake shore before the bells took over?

My mother had an irrepressible energy and enjoyed doing things, staying active, but kept a private space to herself. She spoke not of what she read, what she imagined, what she dreamed of, what she loved. She spoke the negatives of life and my ears recorded them. Each and every story. Each and every rage. Her rants, her raves became mine. Her anguish, her fury mine. Her helplessness, her loneliness mine. That's it—despite gregariousness, loneliness resided within her. Her true self never seemed to make it onto a public page. And the rich humus of that internality lived in the dark, her eyes and their calmness giving it away at times.

I was a quiet girl. I did not know truth could be told. I could hear only others. Who was my sounding board? My doll, Betsy Wetsy? Who my confidante? My stuffed animals—the snake and the crab? Who was my true hearer? Like my mother, I became isolated. I listened for echoes. My own thoughts reverberated, dissipated. *I was my own ears. I was my own ears.*

At eight, sitting in the car, numb as I heard my mother's age-old complaints, I turned to the window. Tense, I squeezed the door handle, wanting exit. Where was I in the glass? A blurred image. No one to mirror me and reflect back unique edges. When I looked into water, it took a long time before I could see, really see, my image. And that image soon gave way to the sandy river bottom. I went on my long beach walks to escape her voice, not in search of my own. Whatever I encountered, I merged with and became. I was a disappearer, a vanisher. I was background noise, something you passed. I sat still and silent and did what I was told until I could run off onto the sand to listen to waves. When did I become my own ears? Twenty-six. Until then, frizzle frazzle, in and out, definite and indefinite, a force not to reckon with. No feet to stand on. My ears full of noise—her noise. My knees in her dirt. My hands planting her seeds, hers.

Truth is, we did not know each other through the words we spoke. Perhaps we knew each other best in our silence, in what we heard in separate rooms: the clack of the dishes as she washed them, the French horn solo she played over and over on the Zenith, the whoosh of the washing machine water flowing out the black tubes, the deep rumble of the dryer, the rapid fire of machine guns on the Roaring Twenties TV Show she tuned to each Thursday night, the loud clack of the clasp on her purse after making a steep purchase, the mumble of her talking to herself in the bathroom, the clang of the lid as she put it onto the sauce pot, Barry Farber's voice droning on the radio each weekday evening seven-eight, and "sleep tight so the bedbugs don't bite" said at the yellow crack of the door before my bedtime. Perhaps I knew her best in the sound of the Dodge station wagon starting up—whether it caught first try or second—

and the scrape of the snow shovel against concrete, and the stamp of her snow boots on the back door mat, and the volume of the news as we drove to the dentist. Her low voice singing *Onward Christian Soldier* and the click of her teacup in the saucer at Aunt Helen's after mass Sundays at St. Luke's Church. The sizzle of Taylor's Pork Roll frying in the pan and the spit of the water boiling spetzeles in the pot. The bonk of plates onto the table calling me to dinner. Had the way the napkins were set told me anything—whether a perfect triangle or one edge off kilter? Or whether the bow of her apron tie was symmetrical? Sounds told me more.

I was my mother's ears interpreting her sounds, so I could know how she felt. Whether I was ok, whether I should feel relief or guilt. Whether I should go outside. Whether I should help or go away. Whether I should listen or not. Whether to look and pretend not to see. Whether to enter the room she was in. The brush clacking on the top of her vanity table meant I could enter her room; the brush banging meant stay out. In this way, she told me everything I needed to know. What sounds of mine did she hear? And what did she know of me because of them?

And so why these tears? We did not *really* know each other. We thought we knew each other, but we never checked out what we thought we knew. We were never sure. She's always said how she'd wished she'd been close to her mother. The grief, the sadness, the loneliness, and the hurt over this relationship was apparent. She tried to know her mother, she told me. She blamed her father; she blamed the too many older brothers. She blamed the too much to do, for her father grew all their vegetables and fruit in their large yard and the kids had to pick the grapes, bag the blackberries, tie the string bean and tomato vines, gather the eggs. Her mother just didn't know how to be close to her kids, my mother told me. And neither did my mother. So she died on her mother's birthday, December 20th—her way of finally becoming close.

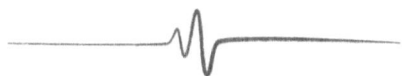

I had heard the story many times of how Mom lost her hearing—the experimental spinal anesthesia, the ether that sickened her profoundly. The fact that she was dropped off at the front of the hospital for the surgery. That she, at age twenty-four, made these decisions without consulting family or friend. When she awoke and the bells were ringing, so loudly she couldn't hear others, well, this part pains me to write. Early on, she told me, the hearing aid batteries were so big she put each one in a pocket of her suit jacket before she went to work. They were the size of batteries that my Uncle Bill, who worked for Bell Atlantic, used in his portable searchlights to work the telephone lines at night. They were heavy and all the world saw that she was disabled and vulnerable. This was hard for her to tolerate.

Years later, she wore hearing aids that her hair hid. Her lobes were large so she could sport earrings nicely. She had the best earrings—the brown leather leaved ones with the veins tooled in; the eggshell white, enameled gold-rimmed leaves; the brown wooden cone shapes, circumference painted red. All clip-ons; pierced meant floozy to her. Many who knew her did not know that she had a major hearing problem.

My mother was beautiful, dark hair and eyes, and I shall always remember her in her silence, for her voice was not pretty. Was it because she could not hear herself that she could not modulate her tone? Her voice was loud, harsh, flat. And when she called me, I often startled. "Hay-lo" in a nasal monotone, emphasis on "Hay" is how she answered the phone, and I see now how she was always raising her voice to talk over something. She struggled to surmount those bells, that cacophony of sound.

In her twenties, she knocked on everyone's door, tying to get help for her hearing problem. Endless numbers of doctors, she told me, which cost a fortune and it was the Depression. One she held in very high esteem— the man who said, Miss Maryott, "You can either hold a gun up to your head and pull the trigger or you can learn to live with it, for there is no help to buy. We've tried everything. Which is it?" When she told the story, she made her hand into the shape of a revolver and pointed it at head. Apparently, he had pointed the *gun* to his head as he delivered his opinion. She was grateful. For her, it was the truth and she stopped chasing shadows.

Later in life, she found fulfillment as a purchasing agent for different corporations. The phone technology had gotten so much better; she was able to adjust the ringer. At home, we had a more elaborate set-up. Phones in almost every room, a dial to modulate loudness, light bulbs that flashed to tell Mom when the phone rang or the front door bell. Flashing lights mounted in the doorways in many colors—red, blue, and yellow. One was in the basement near where she washed clothes, one in the hallway, so she could see from the living room and kitchen, one in her bedroom. Wires hung everywhere—my father's cheap extension cord set-up—but it worked.

I remember once when she was ninety and I was visiting. I came into her bedroom in the morning and she said, "Hold on, Wend, let me dial up." Without her hearing aids, she heard nothing but her own bells. This fact terrified me. I suppose I've always been afraid of losing my hearing. Without sound, was it like floating in space? Dropping down meter after meter of sea, the pressure popping eardrums like scuba diving where all one heard was one's respirator burbling? My mother was a deep sea diver existing in her own depths.

She had a look about her that was both inner and outer and I wonder if that was just her or that was a result of her hearing loss. She was inside and outside at the same time, so I never really felt entirely seen or heard. She existed in a middle world, attuned to her own ethos and to the demands of those around her. And when she was alone, she seemed very, very alone.

I got away with a lot because my mother was unaware. Behind her back, *I got away with murder*, a cliché from the 50s. As a kid, I climbed the steps to her room undetected and stole change from her purse, cursed her "under my breath" right in front of her, opened my bedroom window to escape from my room for an hour or so as a teen, talked on the phone high school weeknights right after she went to bed, eleven to two or three. She took her hearing aids out when she slept and Dad was a sound sleeper.

And who was she really? She who scrubbed the dishes nightly, read books late into the night, and listened to Bing Crosby and Rachmaninoff? Who dropped envelopes of money in the silver plate lined with burgundy felt. Who wore a navy blue veil that dropped down from her navy blue Sunday hat, obscuring her eyes. Who loudly snapped her purse shut at the counter after buying me leotards at the Danskin Shop in Union, New Jersey for my yoga class at the unaffordable Ivy League school I attended. And who vacuumed the hallways each week, cleaned the gutters up until age ninety, and made wreathes of holly each Christmas. She was what she did.

She was a different person from she who walked up the steps of that hospital in her mid-twenties for surgery. In fact, she married shortly after her hearing loss, having vowed, she told me, never to marry. Would I have been born had it not been for her tragedy? She would likely have married but not then. I like wondering about who my mother really was. It's liberating not to feel like I *should* know.

As I wrote earlier, I did not know her. I have all her photos, I have all the stories she told me. I have her jewelry and dishware. I had guardianship over her when she got dementia. I had power of attorney over her money and access to her bank accounts. But who she was will always remain a mystery. I will always be straining to hear who she was and never be quite sure I got it right.

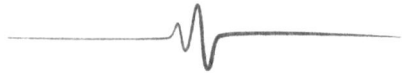

I was my mother's ears. I was my ears always listening *for* her ... to take care of her, protect her. When she swam, she did not wear her hearing aids, so she heard nothing but her own cacophony. Watching her do laps, I patrolled. I could not leave her be. I watched out for her. Made sure her lanes were clear. Did she do this for me? As best she could. Yes, as best she could.

Rage was what I felt if anyone humiliated her. Once Mom and I had gone to buy a clock at the local drugstore and the man at the counter garbled his words when she asked about the price of the clock and the warrantee. "Can you speak up?" she asked. "I can't hear you." He became impatient. "It's year warrantee!" he practically yelled. Her shoulders caved and chin dropped to her chest as she set her white leather purse on the counter and fidgeted with the straps. I had been hiding out in another aisle, pretending to be busy, rebelling—not being my mother's ears for once, not standing next to her to repeat what the man said. My guilt was overwhelming. My rage at this man surging. Couldn't he have responded nicely when she asked him again, noticing her hearing aids? I gave up my rebellion. I went to her aid, stood next to her, lent her my ears.

Funny how deep down I always believed I couldn't live without her, but maybe it was also true that I believed that she couldn't live without me.

Once when I was in high school, my mother actually asked me to drive her to the Beltone Hearing Aid place in downtown Elizabeth. She needed her hearing aids adjusted. My driving her meant I'd miss the first few classes, and since she never sanctioned my being late to school or absent for any reason, I was floored. I felt annoyed because I would have to make up the notes and the work, but I felt humbled, too. I knew my driving her was super important or she wouldn't have asked. She wouldn't have *bothered* me—the problem in our family. We never wanted to *bother* anyone about *anything*. I pulled up in front of Beltone on busy Broad Street, left her off, and pulled into a parking spot to wait. I sat contemplating the situation. Why couldn't she have driven herself, I wondered? Maybe it was unsafe because she couldn't hear. Wow, it suddenly occurred to me that my mother had asked me for a favor! How unusual and odd it felt to feel a little bit necessary and important to her. Tears welled up. Our family was pathetic, I thought. The simple gesture of driving my mother to Beltone such a huge deal. She was *SO* grateful and *SO* sorry she was taking up my time. I felt embarrassed for us. More to the point, I hated us. But looking back, shame was the dominant emotion.

When I was a girl, I remember my mother and me yelling back and forth and sometimes, it was funny. I'd be downstairs looking for a can of peas for her in the pantry, and I'd yell, "No peas!" She's answer, "Please what?" Or I'd say, "I can't find the tomato sauce" and she'd say, "What's lost?" Then I'd go to the base of the stairs and yell up crisply and clearly, "No to-ma-to sauce" and she'd yell back, "Ok, Campbell's Soup then. Alphabet." I was not impatient. I was used to this routine. It was part of life. I was my mother's ears.

DAVID WATTS

My Ellis Experiment: Writing Two Sides of Consciousness

This experiment rose out of my intent to integrate a more associative quality of thinking into the process of making poems. I ended up learning a lot about how the brain works.

As a writer I sometimes wonder how much brainpower I bring to the page, how good I am, beyond the application of craft, at opening pathways to intelligence, to intuition, and to the little wisdoms locked in the organic matrices of the brain.

Process, at some level, involves navigating through all that electro-cellular machinery to assemble some sense of understanding, some authentic engagement with the life experience we have trained ourselves to observe.

We may never know (nor perhaps want to know) the anatomy of these connections. Yet we are in the business of creating a porosity in the membrane that separates us from the deeper currents of human behavior. There are, no doubt, as many ways to accomplish that goal as there are those willing to make the attempt. Even so, technique benefits from a little scientific knowledge, a willingness to experiment, and a whole lot of practice.

My ellis experiment, originally designed to push at these margins, has taken a broader course, evoking a fundamental change in the way my brain orchestrates cooperation between the conscious and unconscious mind during the act of creation.

It's given we only use a fraction of our brains at any one time. Many have said this, including some of my teachers who marveled at how little. Truth is, the brain is constantly active—it's just that part of this massive network seems to be out of reach. Evolution gave us the conscious mind as a problem-solver and though it brings awareness, most brain activity still goes unrecognized.

We might believe we know ourselves pretty well and yet research tells us the unconscious is much larger than the conscious, more powerful, quicker and more active ... without it we could never perform complicated tasks like driving a car or playing a Chopin polonaise. Its speed is phenomenal: whereas the conscious mind processes 40 bits of information per second, the unconscious can perform 20,000,000 bits, somewhere in the range of 500,000 times quicker. Even so, awareness does not extend beyond a shallow cut of this vast terrain.

The brain contains billions of cells grouped into networks that learn, remember, recognize, and organize, and at the same time execute the basic body functions in order to accomplish what we have come to expect of ourselves. Only about 0.01% of that activity is ever experienced in the conscious mind.

Communications between the conscious and unconscious largely go unrecognized. Windows open briefly upon glimpses of the unconscious during REM sleep when dream states reveal what the unconscious has been working on. Flashes of unconscious thought surface during meditation or prayer, or in altered states in which the conscious mind and its tendency to inhibit unconscious representation at the surface have been coaxed into repose.

There are significant differences in brain function. Scientific thinkers are logical and focused. Creative thinkers, distractible and spontaneous. Much of our creative power resides in the unconscious and the more linear thinking conscious mind is a general inhibitor of creative thought.

Long before I knew much about brain physiology I decided to make a departure. I'd been composing poems in a narrative style, and generally pleased with that. Yet, motivated by the idea that beyond the perimeter of poems conceived by the same mind that keeps appointments and integrates science and human behavior at the bedside there was something more to be had—I struck out in search of that wilder, untamed world I wanted in my work.

> *But I know I live half alive in the world,*
> *I know half my life belongs to the wild darkness.*
>
> *- Galway Kinnell*

Trained in hard science I'd already found it difficult to free the controlling grip of a logical, sequential style of thinking to invoke the intuitive, spontaneous reflection necessary for the explorations of poetry. Early on I struggled with the distancing effect of academic language which, at times, sounded more like articles for the *New England Journal of Medicine* than anything remotely resembling art. Insistence upon hard truths, often personal, helped bring back the music and reflective style which made the poems more satisfying:

Words

My father used few words.
He moved fearless from task to task
as if they were meals to be eaten.
Our house grew inglenooks
from the imagination of the carpenter
he became.

From tree limbs of summer
I watched him tote
and saw, driving nails
with the same muscles
that lost baseballs
over West Texas outfields.

Leaves turned.
Snow fell.

All that whiteness
came

Standing
in the emptiness of transition
he spoke
imploring wisdom.
Then, when the inkwell went dry
he reached with great and somber hands
to turn out the light.

—even so, they contained little of that wildness.

Inventiveness, I thought, wasn't making it to the page in large quantities. I had to do something to go beyond the well-trained brain. So I would sit by the fire late in the evening and drift in the direction of sleep then stop half-way and turn back toward wakefulness, far enough to write down what was in my head.

Wild and crazy stuff stepped up:

the petunia at the end of the garden
is the one with the cantilevered system
                                        the cell system

Friday morning and she took me for a walk
and I saw how a basket could be a cell
                                        and a cell a basket

a juggler changing hands

… anything can be lost
in a minute

pouty she said
floating by on her parade float

and nothing mattered but the turn
at the corner of her mouth

These little sums had emerged from somewhere beyond the perimeter of meaning, at least as I knew it. They were clearly willing to risk gobbledygook, yet their energy and wildness pulled me toward another set of realities where a new authenticity, a "smart" thread, ran through, even though the poems themselves were, at times, indecipherable.

I had to trust the process and the product. I had to get over the impulse to reject a thought or image or a wild leap as outlandish. The "Editor" was dead.

Pieces that emerged, which I chose to call poems, were irreverent, quirky, illogical, and confident, as if making sense had little to do with it. Years with this technique and the poems began to change:

> *lunch*
>
> *she served something hot*
> *and rhetorical*
> *said it would make*
> *your cinnamon white*
> *she set the table*
>
> *with lilies*
> *and sexual tension*
> *the way her presence*
> *came into her body*
>
> *the two of them spoke as if*
> *they'd already spoken*
> *all they needed to*
>
> *the sun was in the window*
>
> *something*
> *was just starting up*

—they were now traveling a confident path … but still different.

Consider a poem beginning:

> *my bones*
> *arrange themselves*
> *around everything*
> *I think about …*

As opposed to the more narrative voice:

> *We were sitting in overstuffed*
> *chairs*
> *in a room overstuffed*
> *with people*
> *trying to look casual*
> *and confident …*

The goal of these new offerings, it seemed, was not to make sense out of chaos but to discover within chaos a different sensibility.

And they resisted tinkering. Introduce a revision and there sprang up an opposing force rejecting it. When change was *forced*—even small as a line break or the addition or subtraction of an article—energy dropped, as if the poem had been formed the way it wanted to be formed and to demonstrate disapproval, it unceremoniously self-destructed.

An alternate energy was at work, built upon the manner in which the words linked together. By tinkering, I had produced a power-outage.

Considering how these poems arrived, conflict is not surprising—one part of the brain made them, another part was tempted to edit. The creative part, turns out, was capable of defending itself.

So the idea emerged that the architecture inherent at birth was the holder of the poem's vigor. Whatever the process necessary to the poem's making had been assembled in another world, a world not subject to the rules or operations of the conscious realm.

The question then asked itself: how could a wild thing fly in the open market? Naturally, *I* might like what came forth. It was, after all, my unconscious. Would anyone else?

Well, they did. Sometimes. A few got published here and there with a batting average not unlike that of the usual randomness of the submission process. One won a small recognition in a contest. Another was read on Garrison Keillor's *Writer's Almanac*, two collections are now published, another on its way—a modest achievement, to be sure, yet enough to know the voice had tools for transfer into another person's consciousness.

I gave it a name, this process/this spook/this alter ego: harvey ellis. Harvey from my father's first name. Ellis, my mother's maiden. No caps. No punctuation. The absence of markings and the constriction they impose expanded the perimeter where one might be taken.

The ellis poems are driven by a different motor. If from both styles I select poems on a similar topic and place them side by side, contrasts emerge:

Subject: The Death of My Brother

The Body of My Brother (Watts)

First it belonged to my mother
or seemed to
stuffed into her
like a foot in a sock.
Then it took care of itself,
filling out
into home runs, high jumps.
There were times
it must have been afraid
hiding in a bunker
in South Viet Nam
having happen to it whatever it was
that makes bodies years later
jump out of bed in the middle of the night
not awake

sweating and shouting.
Last time I saw it
it was older than mine,
thinned out
by too many cigarettes
and favors given.
Now they've taken it
from the hospital bed
where it gasped out his last punch line
and put it in a box
that no one will ever see again
though we stand around it
observing gestures even death cannot remove:
head tilt, wry smile,
hands the same as my hands
crossed over his chest
as they never were in life
a few pictures and mementos
scattered around it
as if they were crumbs of a happy life

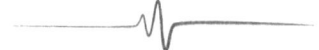

missing Bill (ellis)

your arrival was speckled with departure
the way air is folded
into stone

now the light in the room is like coffee
and the places you have left in the wall
keep changing

October will come again
and go
before your dark eyes land on me

see how the full moon startles the
darkness
on the floor by the window
it will pass over us whether we see it or not

you patience is enormous and has wings
this may come as a surprise to you
but I don't think so

It's dangerous to critique one's own work. So with appropriate reservations, here goes.

Ellis deals with heavy subjects in a lighter, quirky manner, one which allows us not to tarnish under the flame of despondency. Obsession is gone and in its place is a spirit which seems indestructible despite the heavy weight of death or conflict or sorrow. Sentence structure is irreverent and finds itself entirely at the service of the poem and the mood it intends. Breaking conventional syntax, while it is challenging to the ear, allows for a wider range of emotional experiences, some sad, some beautiful, some inexplicable both in meaning and tone. The poem doesn't mind risking meaning altogether, choosing instead an allegiance to feeling.

Subject: mortality and the father and the child ...

Fragment at the Beginning of Something ... (Watts)

My son brings me a stone
and asks what star it fell from.
He is serious,
and so I must be careful, for this
is one of those moments that turns suddenly
toward you, opening
as it turns, as if for a moment
we paused on the edge
of a heartbeat, and then pressed forward, conscious
of the fear that runs beside us
and how lovely it is to be with each other
in the long resilient mornings.

ancestors (ellis)

my ancestors surround me
like walls of a canyon
quiet
stone hard
their ideas drift over me
like breezes at sunset

we gather sticks
and make settlements
what we do is only partly
our own
and partly continuation
down through the chromosomes

my son
my baby sleeps behind me
stirring in the night
for the touch
that lets him continue

he is arranging
in his small form the furniture
and windows of his home

it will be a lot like mine
it will be a lot like theirs

At the root of both poems is an awareness of mortality and the mechanisms we choose to bear the weight of that knowledge. In the first, innocence is compared with wisdom, which incorporates an acceptance of the finite.

In the latter, innocence and knowledge are placed on the overarching scale of time, creating a flicker of permanence in an impermanent world. As such the latter is more optimistic—optimistic, it seems, not out of blind leap but informed by an understanding we cannot quite reach.

To invite the muse writers have employed a variety of imaginative techniques: reading other writers, going to a quiet room, day-dreaming, free-writing, turning on music, off music, induction of trance-like states, the use of alcohol, drugs ... most will acknowledge they need to feel a "shift" in their brain that allows a door to stand open for that highly desired burst of creativity. New dynamic brain studies give us clues about that.

Brain function is sometimes site specific, but more often driven by networks that tend to form and reform. The linear daytime consciousness is driven by an area of relative specificity located in the right prefrontal brain called the Dorsal Lateral Prefrontal Cortex or DLPFC. This area of the brain is humorless, orderly, and inflexible. It is shut down by activities such as jazz improvisation or daydreams but is active during our usual daily lives, balancing checkbooks or deciding which automobile to buy. In PET scans and Dynamic MRI's this nidus of activity turns on during wakeful states and is active when the brain is performing intellectual tasks such as mathematics, debating, playing chess, etc. When the DLPFC is active, creative activity is stifled or at least, dimmed.

As it turns out, highly creative people have lower concentrations of neurotransmitters in their brains and exhibit lower levels of activity in the DLPFC. Instead, a Default Network in the Medial Cortical Area lights up and directs or at least is involved with orchestrating the act of creation. These medial regions of the brain are associated with visual imagery and perception of movement, and they interact freely with deep brain areas connected to emotion. This constellation of regions is flexible and, therefore, highly capable of producing new patterns of thought.

Experiences generated in the Default Network are visually rich and logically loose. But these Medial Cortical Areas seem not to light up when the DLPFC is at work. In order to be creative, the DLPFC has to be attenuated or shut down. When that happens the brain is in a state of "REST" (random episodic silent thought), also referred to as the Default State in which the association cortices are the primary areas that are active and the brain is behaving as a self-organizing system.

Dream states imitate this arrangement. During REM (Rapid Eye Movement) sleep the DLPFC is inactive and other, more disparate regions of the brain light up. Similar patterns of brain electrochemical activity can be produced by meditation, prayer, daydreaming, or quiet reflection. The act of improvisation is rooted here. The ability of the brain to focus, and therefore accomplish difficult intellectual tasks, relies upon the DLPFC. But creative souls are not focused. The advice of the rock group, Talking Heads, when they say "Stop Making Sense" seems, at least some level, to *make sense*. Leonardo da Vinci, arguably one of our most creative individuals ever, was so distractible that, although his notebooks were filled with thousands of creative ideas, he could barely finish a simple task.

The brain has about 100 billion neurons, 300 miles of connections. In it we form networks to perform our tasks of pattern recognition, calculation, identification, etc. Experience changes the network arrangement, which is how we become musicians, artists, mathematicians, poets. These patterns determine the way we think about things, constitute our attitudes and beliefs. This process of pattern setting makes some things easier, some things more difficult.

If the DLPFC dominates, we are serious-minded and tend to approach problems in a concrete manner. But there is an inverse relationship between seriousness and ideas. Paul Valery observed long ago that serious-minded people have few ideas and people with ideas are never serious. Creative ideas push us into uncharted territories and cause us to reorganize ourselves. This requires flexibility, not a characteristic of the DLPFC. But the brain is plastic. When our networks relax, they can change.

We live mostly in our conscious mind. But in the unconscious, associations among prototypes we create to represent things and ideas are looser, better at the task of arranging themselves into new associations. This kind of network is better at solving difficult problems, loosening cognitive tightness into new ways of thinking.

Famous flashes of insight induced by dream states have been associated with important milestones of progress, including some rather significant scientific discoveries. In a dream Mendeleev visualized the elements dropping into a grid and woke to understand the organization of the Periodic Table. Friedrich August Kekule dreamed a snake biting its tail and rolling around, an idea which gave him the structure of the benzene ring. Horowitz and Huang dreamed structures for the laser telescope and laser computing. In literature Mary Shelley and Robert Lewis Stevenson dreamed their characters of Frankenstein and Dr. Jekyll and Mr. Hyde. The list goes on and on. In fact, surveys reveal that roughly fifty percent of artists and musicians rely regularly upon their dreams for inspiration. Awareness, in this case, means shining a light on one's internal state.

Dreams are not only a source of new, imaginative thinking but also a mechanism we use to consolidate learning accessed during the day. Wakefulness is characterized by the use of stored knowledge and a rather limited plasticity, non-REM sleep, by information downloading into stable storage units, and REM sleep as microadjustments in the memory network. The content of dreams is sometimes related to recent learning or, at other times, to a new emotional event. In this way dreams are conducting brain processing. What results is a concretizing of abstract emotional concerns which is why when we are puzzled or confused we have learned to say, "let's just sleep on it," and chances are we will wake in possession of new thinking. We become better at extracting clues embedded in the environment this way. Insofar as we do this consciously we call it intuition.

Einstein says, "The intuitive mind is a sacred gift and the rational mind is a faithful servant. We have created a society that honors the servant and has forgotten the gift."

When we daydream or mind-wander we shut off the DLPFC and activate the Medial Cortical Network. On a chemical level this means that dopamine, the major neurotransmitter, is shut off, deactivating the DLPFC and allowing the Default Network—the problem solving area of the brain—to embellish itself. Logical people have trouble doing that. Creative people have trouble *not* doing that—indeed, they have more trouble deactivating the Default Network in order to get anything done.

Three times in my life a poem hit me fully formed. I had to hurry to write it down because I could tell it was trying to disappear before I could get it on the page. Each time I was blessed with this flash of vision, it happened during the state of daydreaming. After such experience I better understand the common contention of poets that they are not the author of their work but merely the holder of the pen.

Insight requires defocusing. When we are trying to figure something out we use *explicit* processing. We are aware of this. We direct it. *Implicit* processing happens without our knowledge and utilizes vast associative networks that operate under their own power. These networks are inhibited by conscious thought, a process overseen by the DLPFC, so for implicit thinking to occur the dopaminergic tone has to drop far enough to permit associative thought. When someone says we have to stop thinking to be creative, this, at a bio-molecular level, is what they are talking about.

Mozart said, "When I am completely myself, entirely alone ... or during the night when I cannot sleep, it is on such occasions that my ideas flow best and most abundantly. Whence and how these ideas come I know not nor can I force them." Coleridge awoke from a dream (or perhaps an opium haze) to perceive the entire course of the poem "Kubla Kahn" but lost it when his train of thought was broken by the infamous visitor from Porlock. By the time the visitor had left, the vision of Kubla Kahn had evaporated and the poem was never finished.

Even though we are dealing with a part of the mind that is out of our reach we do have recourse. The unconscious is fueled by conscious knowledge. Over time knowledge stored in the unconscious contributes to our ability to play chess, design an art installation, drive a car, or to perform those miraculous feats some can do when large amounts of data are apprehended at a single blink—adding the spots on thirty dominos in 2 seconds, absorbing an entire Beethoven conductor's score flipping rapidly through it. Parts of knowledge-apprehension and decision-making can arrive without linear deduction at each step of the way. And by practice we get better at it. Mozart had to train his unconscious in melody, harmony, and tempo before he could achieve his genius as a composer.

The idea of training the unconscious matches my experience with mr. ellis. At first the offerings were short, no bigger than an isolated thought. Over time they matured and lengthened to include more development, more confluence of ideas, more cross-referencing, as if training could make them more amenable to conscious apprehension. As if training in a commingled experience could inform the unconscious which manner of speaking will land without harsh translation into the conscious world.

> *the soul*
>
> *he stood*
> *in the corner*
> *of the room*
> *untying the bag*
> *around his soul*
>
> *for the soul*
> *wanted to see out*
> *into conversation*
>
> *it was worth watching*
> *the way it would dip*
> *and weave*
> *like tens*
> *of sparrows*
> *flying about the room*
>
> *it was little*
> *about the body*
> *more of the mind*
> *as knowledge*
> *and opinion*
> *danced in circles*

the soul watched and yawned
and almost
went to sleep

the body returned
to its yearning

or this one:

the dead

the dead
walk around
in costumes
imitating
the dead

or what we think of
as dead

ghoulish and apart
into unwhole
body parts

part recognizable
part suggestive
of something
horrible
just so we
can get an
adrenalin surge
that makes us feel
alive

ironic
how the dead
remind us
of that

all curled up
and fishy

To one who participated in the making of these poems it would seem that the unconscious has been fed more substrate to work with and the conscious has become more porous to unconscious thought. Unconscious thinking uses precious few words to accomplish its task. Bukowski said, "An intellectual says a simple thing in a hard way. An artist says a hard thing in a simple way."

Conscious thinking often seems unsure of itself, trying to prove or justify its point of view with supportive data or parallel observations, which, much like scientific writing, must reference itself at every turn. The unconscious doesn't seem to care about detractors, or if it will or will not be understood or praised. It speaks without consideration of correctness or consequence.

My techniques have changed. Instead of writing falling to sleep, a zone best described by Alfred Maury's term the "hypnagogic" state—(it is rumored Benjamin Franklin did this, holding a fork in his hand as he sat at the breakfast table, drifting ... when the fork dropped the clatter roused him and he wrote down what he was thinking)—instead of the hypnagogic state, I have shifted to waking at 2:30 a.m., not turning on the light, writing unseen in the dark, dipping into sleep and dipping back up, careful to remain just under the threshold of forgetting, repeatedly moving back and forth hauling up what little buckets of words that can be fetched. When there was an infant in the house and it was my turn I stumbled upon this technique. You know what I'm saying.

This well-dipping produces something a lot deeper than the "falling-to-sleep" writing, which was the attraction that drew me into this process in the first place. Now that I know a little more about brain physiology I think the reason this is an especially creative window is that the conscious mind has been wiped clean by hours of stage IV sleep followed by progression into REM state during which there is both inhibition of the DLPFC and activation of the microadjusment systems.

I can't do this every night. Such would be counterproductive to my line of work. But as I go merrily along in my daily life, something will tell me the ellis mailbox is filling so I wake up at 2:30 and usually find there are poems waiting. The richness of output runs seasonal but rarely fails. And I write down everything that emerges—I can make no reliable judgments as to what will work later in the realm of its creation. Many choices are good. Linus Pauling says, "The best way to have a good idea is to have lots of ideas." In order to be useful, poems, like ideas, need a certain critical volume.

This process feels like waiting at the shore for parts of an already written manuscript to "bubble up" in sequential pieces across the surface of the invisible, briefly willing to be plucked and assembled. The unconscious, having been prepared by the long unroofing of sleep, is now in the unaccustomed state of finding itself in the driver's seat, pushing its fragmentary offerings across the boundary into the neutral zone where they can be fished into awareness.

Jackson Pollock says that traditional art paints the exterior world, modern art comes from the interior world of the artist. This description seems to parallel the Watts/ellis experience.

Whereas Watts writes narratives that reflect an interior response to an exterior world and, therefore, he might be called an *exteriorist*, ellis writing is almost wholly generated from the interior. He may use external events as prompts but the architecture of thought and the delivery of words and images arise solidly from the interior. He is an *interiorist*.

Poetry is a process of discovery. Stafford says he never starts a poem whose end he knows. To do so, I surmise, would be to allow the DLPFC too much say and the unconscious, not enough.

But if we use pathways in the brain over and over again they become larger, *physically* larger, more efficient, just like copper-wire electrical circuits with greater diameters are less resistant to the conveyance of electricity. The analogy of walking through woods along the same path, beating down the foliage might fit, only here one is causing connections to hypertrophy, to open wider. Finding a pathway, using that pathway, makes it easier to return to the same fishing hole. Now, when I am doing conscious writing of a piece of fiction, or an essay, when I come to a place that needs a metaphor or an image and one does not pop quickly to mind, I can pause and zone-in to a practiced state where I am listening for that "bubbling up" phenomenon and something rare will show itself. I think this means that the practice of opening the portal during near-sleep states has made it possible to dip into that network periodically even when writing fully conscious. The training of a poet might, therefore, benefit from exercises to dilate pathways of exchange across the conscious-unconscious barrier.

Creativity, spontaneous invention, is multiplied by the powerboost we get from engaging the unconscious. The complexity that creativity requires can best be handled by maximum use of large neural networks. Then we can more easily remove our constraints and make new rules.

Most artists and writers have found their own path to the riverbank. My guess is the Language Poets use their own versions of these interior pathways. Perhaps the Symbolists, the Surrealists, and some dream-like filmmakers do as well. My approach has been to work at techniques to dig up the unconscious and use it to perform the act of creation. Such an exercise is useful in unlocking writer's block, breaking out of outdated ruts, transcending self-referential loops that shallow the draft of creative work.

There is a wildness—probably what I was attracted to in the first place—about the unconscious. As linear-driven humans we need that wildness to break out of our narrow patterns into new ideas that have the promise of permanence in a complicated world. Newton had to believe in magic to think of the concept of gravity. So we must periodically suspend science as we know it in favor of knowledge as we may discover it.

If it is true that thinking too hard about craft will cause you to write a bad poem, that talking about stories will impair one's access to deeper meanings, that freezing the kicker will cause him to miss the field goal, then this all may be dangerous doings. But I don't think so. Curiosity about the mind is finally getting some science to help us along.

And so far, the unconscious does not seem to have, nor wish to execute, the kill-shot that pushes the ball wide of the goal posts—the poems are still flowing.

mr. ellis doesn't care who's watching.

CONTRIBUTORS

KATIE AMATRUDA, MFT, EMT, BCETS, is a blogger for the *Huffington Post*. She has written numerous journal articles and chapters for professional publications. Her writing was awarded honorable mentions twice in the Lorian Hemingway Short Story Competition and was a finalist in the Storyville Short Story Contest and the OSA Enizagam Short Story Contest. Her novel "Wizzy-wig" was a semi-finalist in the William Faulkner-William Wisdom Creative Writing Competition.

BAHAREH AMIDI is an Iranian-American poet based in Abu Dhabi. She writes inspirational and spiritual poetry of harmony and peace—what has been described as "poetry of light". She has talked on TEDx in Abu Dhabi. Themes in Bahareh's writing range from exploration of life and its experiences, to finding hope rising above the odds in life, women's and children's issues and world peace and harmony. Bahareh is currently studying the art of poetry therapy at The Institute of Poetic Medicine, USA, and applying the principles of poetic healing through her community service in labor camps and women's groups.

JOAN BARANOW, PhD, is an Associate Professor of English at Dominican University of California. Her poetry has appeared in *The Paris Review*, *Western Humanities Review*, *The Antioch Review*, *The Western Journal of Medicine*, and other magazines. Her poetry has also appeared in *Women Write Their Bodies: Stories of Illness and Recovery*, issued by Kent State University Press. Her book of poetry, *Living Apart*, was published by Plain View Press. With her husband David Watts, she produced the PBS documentary *Healing Words: Poetry & Medicine*.

LEEANN BARTOLINI, PhD, is a Clinical Psychologist and a Professor at Dominican University of California. She was introduced to poetry via a high school teacher's love of Dylan Thomas and her Aunt Sheila Ryan Green's love of reading, writing, and teaching poetry. She has been writing poetry since adolescence, but has recently become a serious student of poetry. She is convinced of the healing aspect of writing and reading poetry and is interested in the intersection of poetry and psychotherapy.

MARISA BOIS teaches yoga and art in Portland, Maine. She is a poet, artist, and lover of life. She is currently exploring how the practices of yoga and writing can help young women develop a positive self-image and a healthy relationship to their bodies. Excerpts from her memoir "Unzip this Skin" have been published in *Ars Medica: A Journal of Medicine, the Arts, and Humanities*, as well as the anthology *Stories of Illness and Healing: Women Write their Bodies*.

FRAN BRAHMI, PhD is a published poet who teaches Narrative Medicine and Critical Thinking Skills to fourth-year medical students. She is also interested in Evidence-Based Medicine and teaches second-year medical students a course in Biostatistics and Evidence-Based Medicine. She volunteers at the Indianapolis Poodle Rescue.

GINA CATENA, MS, CNM, NP is a Certified Nurse-Midwife and Nurse Practitioner who welcomes new life at a busy tertiary care hospital. She believes kindness is intregral to healing, especially in the intimacy of obstetrics and gynecology. Gina enjoys writing about lessons learned from her clients.

ERIC CHANG is a medical student at the University of California, San Francisco. He hopes to have a career in Palliative Care.

CATHARINE CLARK-SAYLES is an internist and geriatrician practicing medicine in Marin County. Her family is from West Virginia but she travelled over much of the United States in a military-brat childhood. After medical school in Colorado she moved to San Francisco in 1979 for training and a stint in the Army. She rediscovered poetry soon after that. Dr. Clark-Sayles has two books of poetry published by Tebot Bach Press: *One Breath* (2008) and *Lifeboat* (2011).

JOANNE M. CLARKSON is the author of three collections of poems: *Pacing the Moon* (Chantry Press), *Crossing Without Daughters* (March Street Press), and *Earth Tones* (Spring Rain Press). Her work appears regularly in small press publications including *Valparaiso Review*, *Caesura*, and *Amoskeag Review*. She has Master's Degrees in English and Library Science but currently works as a Registered Nurse with specialties in Hospice and geriatrics. She is the current Poet-in-Residence with the Pacific Northwest Playwright's Alliance and serves on the Board of the Olympia Poetry Net.

FRAN DORF, MA, MSW, is a psychotherapist and writer, most notably author of three novels, including *Saving Elijah* (Putnam, 2000), which was "inspired" by the 1994 death of Fran's son, Michael, and which a starred *Publisher's Weekly* review called "stunning and spellbinding." Fran's poetry, essays, and articles have been featured in literary journals, anthologies, national periodicals, and online, including *McSweeney's*, *Ars Medica*, *Forbes*, and *Bottom Line*. "Plastic Man" opens Fran's funny/tragic memoir in essays called, *How I Lost My Bellybutton, and Other Naked Survival Stories*. Fran conducts "write to heal" workshops to help people cope with trauma, loss, illness and grief and blogs at www.frandorf.com (The Bruised Muse).

Associate professor at the California Institute of Integral Studies in San Francisco, **JOHN FOX**, CPT, is author of *Poetic Medicine: The Healing Art of Poem-making* and numerous essays. His work is featured in the PBS documentary, *Healing Words: Poetry & Medicine*. He contributed "Healing the Within" to the book, *The Healing Environment* published by the Royal College of Physicians. John presents in medical schools and hospitals including Stanford, Harvard, Shands Hospital in Gainesville, Florida, The Fred Hutchinson Cancer Center in Seattle, and many others places. He is President of The Institute for Poetic Medicine, which offers poetry and healing programs.

MOLLY GILES is the author of a novel, *Iron Shoes*, and two award winning collections of short stories, *Rough Translations* and *Creek Walk*. Among her honors are an NEA, several Marin County Arts Council grants, an Arkansas Arts Council grant, residencies at Yaddo, MacDowell, Villa

Montalvo, and The House of Literature in Greece. She taught creative writing at San Francisco State University for many years. Her best-known "student" is Amy Tan, whose novels she edits.

Originally trained as a hematologist and bone-marrow transplant physician, **DAWN GROSS** began practicing hospice and palliative medicine after her father passed away in 2006. Her work has been published in medical journals, including *Science, JAMA,* and *Annals of Internal Medicine.* She is currently working on a book interweaving the varied experiences of her patients' and father's final months of life. Gratefully married to Dr. Andrew Gross and the proud mother of their three children, Dawn is on the Board of Directors at the Zen Hospice Project and is a physician volunteer with Rotacare Free Clinics.

ERIC HUCKE is a retired United Methodist Minister and now lives in Bemidji, Minnesota. In addition to the ministry, he also worked for twenty years for the American Red Cross Blood Center in St. Paul, where he was an Assistant Director for Donor Recruitment. A 1967 graduate of the University of Minnesota, Eric has studied creative writing at Bemidji State University and is now working toward a low-residency MFA in Poetry at Drew University in Madison, New Jersey.

After a more than 30-year career in teaching and teacher leadership in California, **KAREN KENT**, Ed.D., renewed her interest in writing poetry several years ago by attending a weekend retreat with John Fox. Since then, her poetry has seen her through years of caring for her husband as Alzheimer's Disease claimed his mind, his eventual death in 2012, and two serious illnesses. She leads *Courage to Teach* retreats as a facilitator for the Center for Courage and Renewal and authored the book, *Loving and Caregiving: A journey through poetry and photography*, 2010, Blurb.com.

MARILYN KRYSL's work has appeared in *The Atlantic*, *The Nation*, *The New Republic, Pushcart Prize Anthology*, and elsewhere. *Dinner with Osama* won the Richard Sullivan Prize in 2008 and *Foreword Magazine's* Bronze Prize for best story collection of 2008. *Swear the Burning Vow: Selected and New Poems* appeared in 2009. She has served as Artist in

Residence at the Center for Human Caring, volunteered with Mother Teresa's Sisters of Charity in Calcutta, and worked for Peace Brigade International in Sri Lanka. In Boulder she volunteers with the Lost Boys of Sudan, and is a co-founder of C-SAW, the Community of Sudanese and American Women.

MARTHA LUNNEY is a psychotherapist practicing in San Francisco and the East Bay. She creates art and stories as time allows. She lives with her partner in Richmond, CA.

ADAM LUXENBERG is a third-year medical student at the UC Berkeley-UCSF Joint Medical Program. He writes about his experiences in medical school as part of a weekly writing workshop with his classmates and professors. This piece draws from journal entries written during his first two years of school.

TERRI MASON lives near the Pacific ocean in San Francisco. She writes poetry to expand her notions of possibility. She blogs at http://cancerwell. wordpress.com/ to make sense of her experience and connect with others.

DAWN MGGUIRE, MD, is a neurologist and award-winning author of three poetry collections, including *Hands On* (2002, *ZYZZYVA*) and *The Aphasia Café* (2012, IF SF Publishing). She grew up in Eastern Kentucky and was educated at Princeton University, Union Theological Seminary, and the Columbia College of Physicians and Surgeons. She is the 2011 winner of the Sarah Lawrence/Campbell Corner Language Exchange Poetry Prize, awarded for "poems that treat larger themes with lyric intensity." McGuire is Professor of Neurology at Morehouse School of Medicine, and divides her time between Atlanta and the San Francisco Bay Area.

SUSAN MOLDOW recently completed a hospital chaplaincy program of clinical pastoral education. She currently works in the field of spiritual care and chaplaincy. She has a B.A. *cum laude* from Wesleyan University, an MBA from UCLA's Anderson School of Management, and a Masters in Gerontology from San Francisco State University. She completed a program of Jewish literacy and leadership through the Wexner Heritage Foundation, and has served on nonprofit boards and committees in the

San Francisco Bay Area. Her fiction and nonfiction have been published in *Narrative* magazine.

MEG NEWMAN, MD, worked at SFGH, as a clinician, from 1984 until 2008. She joined the AIDS Division in 1994 as a clinician-educator, developed and directed many programs for patients and trainees and was sidelined prematurely due to spinal disease. Meg was a profoundly devoted and much beloved clinician, educator, and colleague. She began writing in the spring of 2010, is currently engaged in learning the craft of writing, and appreciates the transformative nature of self-expression through the written word. She lives happily in San Francisco with her partner, Sherry Boschert, and their ever-amusing ocicat, Alli.

ALICA OSTRIKER has published thirteen poetry collections, including *The Book of Seventy*, which received the 2009 National Jewish Book Award for Poetry. *The Crack in Everything* and *The Little Space: Poems Selected and New, 1969-1989*, were both National Book Award finalists. As a critic, Ostriker is the author of *Stealing the Language: the Emergence of Women's Poetry in America*, as well as several books on poetry and on the Bible. Ostriker is Professor Emerita of Rutgers University, and teaches in the Low-Residency Poetry MFA Program of Drew University.

SARAH PARIS is a Swiss-American writer, poet, editor and photographer. She lives in San Francisco.

JENNY QI is a PhD student in biomedical sciences at UCSF, which is a fancy way of saying she's putting off adulthood by pretending to cure cancer. She has previously published poems in various journals, including the *Vanderbilt Review*, *Tabula Rasa*, and *The Quotable*. When not in the lab, she continues to read and write existentially sad poems, blogs with absurd frequency, and draws science cartoons for the *Synapse*, the UCSF newspaper.

RUTH SAXEY-REESE teaches poetry writing at Boise State University and at non-profit literary organizations in Southwest Idaho. She has conducted research into the therapeutic value of expressive writing, and is currently in the process of establishing Boise's first writing group for combat veterans. Her work has appeared in several journals including *Chiron Review*, *Nerve Cowboy*, and *Rattle*, and has twice been nominated for the Pushcart Prize.

NINA SCHUYLER's novel, *The Painting*, was nominated for the Northern California Book Award and was named a Best Book by the San Francisco Chronicle and a "fearless debut" by MSNBC. Her second novel, *Accidental Birds*, which takes place in 1924 Berlin, will be published in 2012. Her short stories have been nominated for a Pushcart Prize and Best New American Voices. She is fiction editor at Able Muse and teaches creative writing at the University of San Francisco.

A member of the Squaw Valley Community of Writers, **DAVID SCRONCE** holds an MFA from the writing seminars at Bennington College. His poetry chapbook, *Letters to Liam*, was published by Red Berry Editions (2009). His work has appeared or is forthcoming in *5AM*, *Bennington Review*, *Cloud View Poets*, *Hayden's Ferry Review*, *Poetalk*, *The Portland Review*, *RUNES*, *Salamander*, *Sierra Nevada Review*, and online at *Four and Twenty*, *PoetryBay.com*, and *ChaparralPoetry.net*.

NORMA SMITH worked for the better part of forty years in hospitals and other health care institutions, before her retirement. She has served for several years on a medical center ethics committee. She lives and writes in Oakland, CA, and facilitates writing groups on health and healthcare-related themes. Contact: nsmith@igc.org

DEBORAH STEINBERG holds a BA in Creative Writing from Bard College and an MA in English Literature from the University of Bordeaux, France, where her thesis focused on the intersection of literature and medicine. During her seven years in Bordeaux, she taught English, sang in bands, edited a 'zine, and refined her sense of joie de vivre. She currently lives the good life in San Francisco, where she serves as Director of Artist Services at WomenArts and Managing Editor at Red Bridge Press. She also sings in the acappella group Conspiracy of Venus. Website: http://deborahsteinberg.wordpress.com

SUZANNE TAY-KELLEY received her first paycheck from writing as a reporter for the *Los Angeles Times*. After nearly a decade in journalism she entered healthcare as a management consultant with PricewaterhouseCoopers and Kaiser Permanente before becoming a cardiac and surgical oncology nurse at UCSF and the SF VA Medical Center for seven years. She cared for rheumatology patients as a nurse practitioner for a year. Her current passion is palliative care. She enjoys her patients, travel, photography, and family most of all. She and husband Myles are celebrating their 25th anniversary in 2013 despite his recent diagnosis of corticobasal degeneration.

JULIANNA WATERS, LCSW, has been a writer/psychotherapist in private practice in Portland, Oregon for twenty years. She specializes in working with individuals contending with illness, pain, and death. She is an award winning singer-songwriter, accomplished poet, and is currently working on her first novel. She is the founder of both The Poetry Wheel Series and the Medicine Song Workshop. She facilitates personal and creative retreats throughout the west.

PAUL WATSKY's poetry collection *Telling The Difference* was published in 2010 by Fisher King Press. He is co-translator with Emiko Miyashita of Santoka (Tokyo, PIE Books, 2006). Among the journals where he has work recently published or forthcoming are *The Carolina Quarterly*, *Smartish Pace*, *Interim*, and *Permafrost*.

DAVID WATTS' second book of stories, *The Orange Wire Problem*, along with *Bedside Manners*, forms a body of work which explores the intricacies of the art of medicine. He has published four books of poetry and a CD of "word-jazz." He is an NPR commentator on *All Things Considered*, a producer of the PBS program *Healing Words: Poetry and Medicine*, a gastroenterologist at UCSF, and a classically trained musician. A volume of avant-guard poetry, *sleep not sleep*, was published under his pseudonym, Harvey Ellis, by Wolf Ridge Press.

Writer, public speaker, and workshop facilitator, **WENDY PATRICE WILLIAMS** is an accomplished poet with two chapbooks, *Some New Forgetting* and *Bayley House Bard*. Her blog, myincision.wordpress.com

— Living in the Aftermath of Infant Surgery, features inspiring words of healing, highlighted with original artwork, and articles that help people cope with early trauma and PTSD. An excerpt of her memoir manuscript, *The Autobiography of a Sea Creature*, appears in *The Healing Art of Writing* (UC Press). *Turning the Page: Poems of Trauma, Healing and Transcendence*, which Wendy is co-editing, will be published by Fearless Books later this year.